To Brenda

Happy Reading

2018

Acknowledgements

To my daughter, Ariel, who first heard this faerie-tale I had bouncing around in my head when it was still in its infancy. And to my son, Kristopher, who has yet to hear it.

I further want to acknowledge my editors who helped me throughout my writing process; Ms. Connie Williams of Lamesa, TX and Ms. Clare Keogh of Dublin, Ireland. I couldn't have done it without you. You both are truly brilliant. Thank you!

To Chef Jacques Torres, M.O.F. *(Meilleurs Ouvriers de France),* watching your show, *Dessert Circus with Jacques Torres*, many years ago was truly an inspirationally-delicious experience. And to my new friends at the Chocolate Gallery, right here in downtown Bryan, TX: Executive Chocolatier, Chef Joshua Neubauer and his lovely wife, Executive Pastry Chef –Chef Ciana Neubauer, I am forever grateful for your loving kindness and support.

To the wonderful people of Wehrheim, Germany (aka Apfeldorf), and to my friend, Claudia Löhr and her wonderful family. Thank you so much for your hospitality and friendship over the years. And for the marvelous and memorable walks in the November snow through the forest of Cratzenbach.

And lastly,

To all the children of the world who dare to dream wonderful, creative, and often times impossible dreams. It is you, my dear ones, who will one day change the world!

- B.W. Van Alstyne

The Sweet Adventures of Henry P. Twist

B. W. Van Alstyne

THE SWEET ADVENTURES OF HENRY P. TWIST

This is a work of fiction. All of the characters, names, incidents, organizations, and dialogue in this novel are either the products of the author's imagination or are used fictitiously.

iUniverse books may be ordered through booksellers or by contacting:

iUniverse
1663 Liberty Drive
Bloomington, IN 47403
www.iuniverse.com
1-800-Authors (1-800-288-4677)

ISBN: 978-1-4917-5199-2 (sc)
ISBN: 978-1-4917-5200-5 (hc)
ISBN: 978-1-4917-5198-5 (e)

Library of Congress Control Number: 2014921957

Print information available on the last page.

iUniverse rev. date: 04/20/2015

Prologue

It was harvest time again, and the residents of Apfeldorf were extremely busy making last minute preparations for the Apple Blossom Festival. Every year for generations a beautiful maiden of the city was chosen to be crowned the Apple Blossom Queen for one whole year. Amongst the hustle and scurry of festival preparations, the city itself was getting a grand makeover. A new hotel and fancy apartment buildings were being built to handle the influx of new residents and visitors that came each year. An old cobblestone road, a leftover remnant of the past, wound its narrow way through the village ending right at the steps of the Red Town Hall. Even the "Red" Town Hall, which sat in the very center of the city, was getting a new look.

On the whole Apfeldorf remained serene; a sleepy little hamlet nestled in a valley twenty miles north of a large, bustling metropolis. Houses with even rooflines boasting meticulously manicured lawns and beautiful well-kept gardens sat on quiet little streets. Apple orchards dotted the verdant valley, with most of their fruit going to a very prominent maker of schnapps: a kind of sweet brandy made from the pressings of fermented fruit.

But behind the façade of festivals, countless renovations and newly constructed buildings, lay a fifty-year-old scandalous mystery Apfeldorf has yet to forget.

The epicenter of the scandal took place at a factory called Brackmeyer Sweets. Though the facts of that case are somewhat vague, so-called eye witnessed accounts led to a fantastical tale that continues to dance in the mind of Apfeldorf folk. A tale that few are willing to tell. A tale that involves an extraordinary pastry chef named Henry P. Twist, whose disappearance is unsolved to this day, despite many rumours that he was spirited away by faeries. And that Charles B. Brackmeyer Jr., son and heir to the world famous Brackmeyer Sweets Empire, whose new title as president coupled with his embittered struggle to gain total control of an outdated factory, forced this money driven young man to stop at nothing to become "the richest, most powerful man in Germany."

CHAPTER ONE

The Vanishing Old People

Apfeldorf, Germany – 1964

The Brackmeyer Sweets factory was the crown jewel of Apfeldorf for many years. It stood in the center of the city, some fourteen stories tall and employed over four thousand people, which included people from neighboring towns. A large, black iron gate guarded the entrance and was flanked by two huge stone walls that wrapped around the perimeter. On a corner opposite the factory sat a tiny shop with bright yellow awnings. On these awnings, inscribed in bold, black lettering, were the words: **Brackmeyer's Konditorei.**

Every morning the little shop was crowded with loyal patrons, each scrambling to make their way to the counter to order their favorite victuals before scurrying off to work or school. By mornings end, nothing of the breakfast pastries was left. In the afternoons a replacement of a variety of hearty breads, decadent cakes, sweet and savory pies, custards and countless other confections lined the shelves. These too disappeared with the same insane rapidity as that morning's stock. A long underground tunnel connected the factory to the tiny shop. This made it easy to transport goods to the shop from the factory's massive kitchen.

The factory kitchen was indeed enormous. Long conveyor belts, one of two automated modern conveniences allowed in the factory's kitchen, laden with boxes and filled with chocolates or some other sweet moved swiftly along passing by workers who inspected and covered them with their personal lids before another machine sealed them completely in clear plastic wrapping. The finished boxes were then placed into much larger boxes to be shipped elsewhere. Many of these boxes had large 'Air Mail' and 'Ship by Air' stickers on them with names of faraway places like London, New York, Paris, Sydney and Bangkok.

Several metal cauldrons, some as big as a two car garage, simmered away, their lids clanging and clanking up steam. Two of them with pour spouts contained hot melted chocolate or caramel. Two people dressed in what looked like space suits designed to withstand very intense heat, watched over them as they bubbled. Four hundred workers busied themselves stirring the contents of the other large cauldrons. One group made puff pastry, while another group made cream filling. Still others worked under great metal lamps, bending and pulling, twisting and shaping colored sugar into different shapes such as ribbons or flowers. Some workers pulled and wrapped taffy. Some dipped fruit into chocolate or poured chocolate into moulds, while twenty people stood along a great marble table kneading, rolling and shaping dough into pie shells to be filled almost immediately with some sort of fruit or cream filling. Forty large ovens were lined up against a great brick wall of the kitchen where five bakers, assigned to work eight ovens each, constantly put in and took out baked goods.

Brackmeyer Sweets was a well-oiled machine that ran without as much as a hiccup for many years. Both the factory and the tiny shop were diligently overseen by its founder, Charles Benjamin Brackmeyer Sr., a very kind and gentle man with a marvelous knowledge of baking. But as the years rolled along and the founder's health and age got the better of him, it became more difficult for him to carry on the long hours he was so accustomed to.

On a cold December morning, the founder called a meeting. Flanked by his son and his master pastry chef, Henry Twist, the elder Brackmeyer addressed his loyal employees for the very last time.

"My dears," croaked the aged, old man, leaning on the railings of the kitchen's balcony for support, "it is with a heavy heart that I must step down as acting president of this company. As most of you know, my son, Charles, has come of age. Tomorrow morning, he will become acting president of the factory."

This announcement was met with fear, followed closely by panic. Charles B. Brackmeyer Jr., had to be the wickedest man in the world. Nobody liked him at all. In fact they all hated him. He had very pale skin, short jet black hair and a sharp nose like a bird's beak. He wore a black tailor-made suit, which made him look even paler by comparison. Henry thought he looked more like a malnourished bird of prey. But the most unsettling thing about Brackmeyer were his eyes: they were dark, cold, uncaring eyes that reflected an ominous motive coiled behind the smile.

The younger Brackmeyer stepped forward clasping his hands before him and surveyed his workforce. His thin lips curled in what seemed like more of a sneer than a smile to all watching. "I am looking forward to continuing the long tradition of excellence this company is known for," he said importantly. "Times are indeed changing, and soon, so must our methods. We shall be ready to meet these changes, head on! Ready to adopt new and improved ways of production. Let us, therefore, go forth into this new century setting the bar ever higher as we go!" He stepped back behind his father. There was a smattering of confused applause at this pronouncement.

Henry and the other employees looked around at each other utterly speechless, for no words could convey the troubled storm they feared was to come. A hint, however, came during the walk-through of the factory's massive kitchen, as the new president made his intentions quite plain to all within earshot.

"Consider for a moment, father," said Brackmeyer in an cunningly, oily voice, "the money we'd save if we got rid of some of the dead weight and brought this factory up to date. We would boost our production by fifty percent within the first year."

It was well known by all that Brackmeyer hated his father's antiquated methods of production and tried at every turn to convince his father to bring the factory 'up to date.' Though every new attempt at mechanization was met with hostility by the founder, who believed that machine-made cakes and pastries tasted flat and stale like cardboard. Over the whizzing hissing and clanking of steam jacketed kettles workers heard the founder exclaim:

"As long as I am alive no machine will ever make as much as a muffin in my factory!"

"Doddering old fool. We'll see about that!" mumbled Brackmeyer furiously as he stormed towards the exit.

By the New Year the factory had learned that its founder, Charles B. Brackmeyer Sr., had been sent to live the rest of his days in a retirement home in the German countryside. Less than a week after that, a rumour began to circulate around the factory that the founder, along with ten other old people, had mysteriously disappeared in the night from the retirement home. A week later, several more had vanished from their beds. A massive hunt for the old people was launched and after an extensive two-day search of the surrounding area the police turned up nothing. Where had they all gone? It was as if they all had just vanished into thin air. Though the founder was missing, it was presumed he was still alive, and by law a person had to be missing for several years (seven to be exact) before they could be pronounced officially 'dead.'

So Brackmeyer had to wait. And wait he did, for seven long years. Just when it seemed that he could not get any nastier, the president managed to surprise them all with new levels of vindictiveness. He implemented longer work hours with less pay. Lunch breaks were cut down to fifteen minutes instead of the usual half-hour. He even took to stalking the corridors of the factory, jumping out from around corners, determined to catch people in the act of skiving off so that he could fire them on the spot.

Then, exactly seven years to the day of the disappearances, word spread like wildfire throughout the entire factory that the founder was ...

"Dead, are you sure?" came a high-pitched voice from an office door, which stood ajar in the main corridor.

"Heard it for myself this morning," said another voice in rich, dark tones. "It's been seven years since his disappearance and not one clue to his whereabouts."

"But what does this mean?" said the high pitched voice, frantically.

"I'll give you one guess," said the other, lowering his voice, "There won't be a person over forty left in the factory now that Brackmeyer's fully in charge. You mark my words."

In the days that followed that fateful pronouncement, the workers waited anxiously, waited, as they say, for the 'other shoe to drop.' A terrible gloom hung about the place like a very bad cold. Everyone went about their day never really knowing when exactly the change would come.

But come it did, swiftly and without fan-fare. The ink had barely dried of the founder's death certificate when memos, hundreds of them, addressed to a specific person, or to persons over the age of sixty-five in every department. It seemed that no one could escape what was to come, what was already here, not even Brackmeyer's celebrated master chef.

CHAPTER TWO

An Unpleasant Journey

Henry Peppermint Twist looked balefully out of the window of the bus watching great stretches of narrow road wrap itself around large parcels of vacant land, disappearing behind him. He watched miserably as the city he loved sank slowly below the horizon, wondering if he would ever see it again.

He pressed his forehead against the cold, hard glass, wanting desperately to slip right through it. He knew he couldn't. He knew he was being silly for even imagining such nonsense. But the thought of escaping his new fate offered him a modicum of pleasure all the same. To distract him from his unpleasant thoughts, Henry fixed his eyes on something other than the horizon line or the black tar road. A herd of cows came into view. He watched them as they grazed contentedly in a grassy field, their tails swishing this way and that as they rid themselves of the pesky flies that swirled above them in the hot summer sun. The scene changed abruptly and Henry's eyes fell upon a small group of children kicking a ball around in a vacant field. *"To be young again,"* Henry thought to himself. He sat back in his seat feeling tired and run down, and very, very old. He wished for the very first time in many years that he could somehow turn back the hands of the clock.

Henry was a tall, slender man of sixty-five with chocolaty-brown eyes that had in recent years, twinkled vibrantly whenever he spoke. His hair, once full, brown and as thick as treacle, was now completely silver and resembled cotton candy spun by the wind and placed whimsically upon his head. His face, once having given the appearance of eternal youth, in spite of his years, was now marked with lines and creases. The spark that once burned so brightly was almost lost behind his eyes.

Henry looked at his hands. These were once good, strong, capable hands. Now they had a careworn, overworked look to them. They were spotted and wrinkled with age. He put them back on his lap and gazed out his window as a new feeling flushed through him: regret.

He had no family. No wife or children to care for, or to care for him. His parents were only a memory now. He had no siblings he could call upon, or go to for help. As Henry tried to find a brighter side to his situation; he found nothing.

"Forty five years …," he muttered miserably to himself, pounding a gnarled fist into the palm of his other hand.

For forty-five years Henry worked as the Master Pastry Chef for Brackmeyer Sweets. "Who would want to hire an old pastry chef?" He wondered. The world had changed so much around him. Baking was his whole life. Lost in thought, he recounted his last day at the factory.

He was in his office about to flop down in a chair at his desk (he had just heard the news about the founder and was trying desperately to steady the panic that was swelling up inside him) when a tall boy came bouncing merrily in. . . .

"Hi Henry," said the boy brightly. He carried several small white boxes and sat them on a clear patch of desk. "I've got something for you."

"Hi Wally," said Henry, trying hard now to sound normal and look more cheerful.

Walter Hingle (Wally as he liked to be called) was a tall skinny, bespectacled boy of eleven. He had dark brown hair the color of molasses, much like Henry's used to be, and brown eyes the shade of caramelizing sugar after it has been brought to a rolling boil -- just moments before you add the cream. Every day after school Wally would come to work at the factory to see if Brackmeyer had any odd jobs he needed done. When Wally wasn't doing that, he was usually found stalking around in the kitchen. Henry enjoyed having Wally around. He asked a lot of questions and his enthusiasm about baking was very infectious. It kept Henry sharp and made him feel young.

"What's that?" asked Henry, warily eyeballing the piece of paper that lay on top of the boxes.

"A memo from Brackmeyer's office," said Wally, popping a piece of candy into his mouth.

Henry took the memo apprehensively. Under normal circumstances he wouldn't have worried about what was written on the little yellow piece of paper, but these weren't normal circumstances. Not after all he had heard, and all the rumors and gossip. A feeling of impending doom swept over him as he read the note:

Dear Mr. Twist,

Your presence is requested on a very important matter. Please come to my office at 3:15pm, sharp! DO NOT BE LATE!

Yours truly,

Charles B. Brackmeyer Jr., President.

Henry looked at his watch. He had exactly five minutes to make it to the fourteenth floor. He excused himself to Wally and left his office, half walking, and half running by several small offices on his way to the elevators. Mid way down the corridor, a door stood ajar. He could just see inside as a man with gray hair packed books and other personal effects into a box. Another door revealed a silver haired woman who sobbed uncontrollably over the telephone. Closer to the elevators a woman with salt and peppered hair and very thick glasses was steadily throwing things pell-mell into several old shopping bags in her office, stopping every now and again to wipe at her nose. Henry entered the elevator, his heart beating wildly in his chest. He closed his eyes and took a couple of deep calming breaths and tried very hard not to think about what was in store for him.

Suddenly the doors of the elevator chimed opened, and Henry quickly stepped out into a very large, overly polished, marbled-floored lobby. Dark wood panels covered every square inch of wall space. Photographs, portrait after portrait of the beady eyed Brackmeyer hung in gold-leaf frames and disappeared down a long hall that led towards Brackmeyer's office. In an adjacent room, off the lobby, armchairs of carved mahogany and brocade cushions were arranged beside an overstuffed divan of matching upholstery. Tiffany lamps lit the small waiting room in soft white light, casting shadows into empty spaces creating a relevant darkness.

"Go right in Mr. Twist," came an angelic voice as Henry stepped from the elevator. The voice belonged to Katie Brumwell, a very pretty girl of twelve. She had long blond hair and her bright blue almond shaped eyes twinkled vibrantly. She also happened to be Brackmeyer's niece. Katie had come to live with her maternal grandparents, Charles and Sophia Brackmeyer, when her own parents had died. By age ten her uncle had put her to work after school as his personal assistant. Henry knew this of course as Wally happened to be the eyes and ears of the factory; he was also very fond of Katie and she him.

Katie's desk perched next to the elevator doors. The simple pine secretariat clashed with the recently added opulent surroundings of luxurious woods, plush couches and decorative settees. Henry smiled at its old fashioned ink pot, a fitting reminder of the missing elder Brackmeyer's old fashioned ways. It made him think of the kind of desks used by teachers in a public school. Some of the nervousness left him as he surveyed her situation. He felt sorry for her, after all, she had to deal with Brackmeyer on a daily basis.

"Good luck," said Katie in a whisper. She gave Henry an encouraging smile that lit up her delicate porcelain face. Henry started nervously down the hall, which seemed to lengthen with his every step. He also noticed that the light seemed to grow dimmer as he neared the end of it. His stomach did a couple of somersaults as he approached Brackmeyer's office. He found the door ajar. Gathering up what little courage he thought had left him, he knocked.

"Come in!" boomed a voice from within. Henry entered, his knees knocking. Brackmeyer was sitting behind his desk in a large burgundy leather swivel chair smoking a big, fat cigar that filled the room with thick heavy smoke.

"Well don't just stand there gawking, man," snapped Brackmeyer, impatiently, "Come in and sit down!"

Henry did as he was told. Brackmeyer took another draw from his cigar and blew smoke in Henry's direction as he watched him take his seat in a very large chair, which seemed to swallow him up. Silence filled the room as Brackmeyer shuffled through a few papers on his desk. Henry shivered. The room, with the exception of Brackmeyer's desk, was in complete darkness and very cold. Thick velvet curtains that hung from ceiling to floor were drawn shut. A chill, the kind that clings to the skin and goes right to one's bones, hung in the air. He shivered again and looked around for something to distract himself. He spotted a glass ball resting on a stand at the edge of the desk. He picked it up to look at it more closely.

"Hey, that's mine!" shrieked Brackmeyer. Startled, Henry fumbled almost dropping it. "Put that down at once! I don't like it when people put their hands on my stuff. Hasn't anyone ever taught you not to mess with things that don't belong to you?"

Startled by the selfish behavior of the president, Henry placed the small glass orb back on the desk. Brackmeyer continued to eye him for several moments, scrutinising his every movement through narrowed eyes. Silence resumed as Brackmeyer's attention turned once again to shuffling more papers around in his hands. After several seconds more of this he spoke again.

"Here we are, Henry P. Twist. What does the P. Stand for?"

"Peppermint," Henry replied proudly, puffing his chest out a bit.

Henry's mother had indeed named her only son after the infamous weed. It was quite amazing, Henry thought, how many uses she found for it. She used the leaves in salads, and in making tea, and of course in making candy. The entire house smelled of peppermint. Henry's mother often made essential oil from the leaves, which she used on a cotton ball (just a drop) to keep the mice away. It was her favorite plant.

"You have got to be kidding!" said Brackmeyer incredulously, interrupting Henry's trip into the past. His hard eyes narrowed again as he scrutinised Henry. "No, I can see you're not."

Henry frowned. He always had to put up with people teasing him about his middle name. But after a while, he found he didn't care. He was proud of it and he wasn't going to let Brackmeyer or anyone else belittle him about it. He scowled at the president, who had already returned to reading what was on the documents he had before him.

"It says here that you've been with the company for forty-five years?"

"Yes, sir," said Henry, his frown vanishing, and now sitting forward on the edge of his chair. "Actually, technically, it's been forty-five years, eleven months and …" he broke off, catching Brackmeyer's unconcerned gaze, and sank quietly back in his chair.

"Yes, well a man your age needs to start thinking of spending the golden years of his life vacationing in Spain, or on a cruise or wherever you old people like to go,"

Brackmeyer stood, puffing ferociously on his cigar which had gone out. He stopped talking to relight it.

Henry's smile faded. "I'm being fired, Sir?"

"Fired?" said Brackmeyer, his brow raised in feigned confusion. "Not fired, Henry, I'm talking retirement, full benefits, the works!" He pushed a button on his desk and spoke into a little box Henry mistook for a stereo speaker. "Katie, bring in Mr. Twist's retirement packet right away!"

Henry squirmed uncomfortably in his seat as little pearls of sweat formed on his forehead, like water collecting on a leaf. *"But of course,"* Henry thought. He knew this day had to come, for shortly after the founder was officially pronounced 'dead,' Brackmeyer wasted no time taking total control of the company. Katie walked in and placed a large envelope on Brackmeyer's desk. She turned to see Henry's discomfort and her eyes filled with tears. She walked quickly from the room, closing the door with a sharp snap behind her.

"Now then, Henry," said Brackmeyer, unceremoniously and in his most business-like sounding voice, "I think you'll be very impressed by the company's generous retirement plan, which includes lodging at our very own retirement facility." He handed Henry the envelope. "Just think of it, no more coming in early and leaving late. You'll be able to sleep in, play shuffleboard or bingo and a lot of other things a person your age likes. You do like bingo, don't you, Twist?"

Henry found that he couldn't speak. It felt like the roof of his mouth had been cemented shut with Hazelnut butter. He nodded his answer instead.

"Good!" boomed Brackmeyer, "It's all settled, then."

"But I'm not ready to retire, Henry said, finding his voice at last. He stared into Brackmeyer's cold, hard eyes and watched them roll. "Please sir, this job means everything to me ..." But Brackmeyer cut across him abruptly,

"That will be all Mr. Twist," he said dismissively. "That will be all!" and he began to shuffle papers around on his desk, feigning busyness.

The Bus gave a sudden jolt as the driver applied the brakes, jolting Henry out of his horrible reverie. An overwhelming sadness, mingled with fear, threatened to overtake him as he descended the steps. As the door slammed shut behind him and his only means of transport drove away and rounded a corner, Henry wished a new wish: that he could have left all of his worries behind him on that bus.

CHAPTER THREE

A Restful Retreat

A light breeze of hot air rustled Henry's already wind-blown hair. He surveyed the surrounding countryside. Large parcels of vacant land surrounded by a vast, dark forest made up the tiny town of Cratzenbach. A row of houses sat upon a hill in the distance. Although he was familiar with the town, he hadn't actually been to the area since his parents died. It was usually during the winter months that the Twist family would take an hour-long walk through the forest to the Eichelbacher Hof, another ancient relic of the past saved by the Hessian State Office of Historic Monuments. It was restored and turned, delightfully, into a restaurant, a wonderful treat after a long walk in the deep snowy forest. But Henry wasn't here for the hour-long walk. At first glance he thought he got off at the wrong stop. Pulling out the envelope containing his retirement information, Henry checked the address and photograph on the brochure against what he saw. And what he saw made his stomach drop a notch. The picture showed a very beautiful piece of property with pristine manicured grounds surrounded by a vast forest. Big bold lettering on the cover pronounced, 'The Countryside Retirement Home: a restful retreat.' Henry looked up from the brochure. There wasn't anything sunny, pristine or restful looking about this place. Paint peeled in large sections from the exterior walls. Several tiles were missing from the roof and the windows looked as though they hadn't been washed in a hundred years. To Henry the building seemed to be slowly crumbling away and looked like anything but a restful retirement retreat.

The grounds too were in a terrible state. There were great patches of brown grass spotting the lawn, and in some areas there was no grass at all. Henry continued to look at the brochure. He checked the photographs against the real thing. His frown deepened with every turn of the page. *"Where were the elegantly arranged flowerbeds, and beautifully trimmed trees?"* he wondered as he stared down at the brochure then up at the landscape. Except for the forest in the background, the property seemed to be stripped bare of them.

He chanced another glance at the brochure. In it was a photo of a beautifully kept garden maze with hedges ten feet tall, and in the center, a white gazebo with blue trim. He could only imagine what that looked like now. Absolutely appalled at what was to be his new home, Henry gathered up his courage, along with his suitcase, and made his way up the uneven walkway and entered the building, hoping that the interior was much better.

As Henry stood at the front door, the heavy smell of disinfectant and mothballs greeted his nostrils making his eyes water and his nose sting. He stepped over the threshold taking in everything from the dingy gray curtains in the sitting room to the overly polished floors. "At *least it was clean,"* he thought dismally. It was indeed just as dreary and depressed looking as the outside. Even the residents looked tired and woebegone, as if all the happiness and energy were sucked out of them through a straw. Most of them just sat in one place in the sitting room, dressed in their pajamas, bathrobes, and slippers. The ones that were not seated moved at a snail's pace back and forth, from one place to the next. Would this become him in a few years? He shivered a bit; and felt as if the temperature had dropped a few degrees. And then he spotted the source of his chills. An enormous portrait of Charles B. Brackmeyer Jr. was hanging on the wall behind Henry. He gave another involuntary shiver as the painted image looked imperiously down upon him, arms folded. It gave Henry the awful feeling that his every move was being closely monitored. Even as a painting Brackmeyer's cold demeanor emanated outward and enveloped you like a wintry morning. And then something clicked in Henry's mind.

"But of course," Henry thought to himself. *"It was Brackmeyer's plan all along. Force people over the age of 65 into this retirement facility to get at their pensions."* a clever idea he had to admit, scowling up at the portrait once more as he made his way to the nurse's station.

A very plump nurse with a very round, pink face sat eating her lunch behind a circular counter. He stood watching her for a moment, his mouth agape as she hungrily shoved the last of what looked like a submarine sandwich into her mouth. The nurse chewed ferociously, her cheeks bulging like two pink balloons, stopping only for a second to take a couple of large swigs from a two-liter bottle of an orange diet soft drink. She swallowed hard and after a rather uncouth display of belching, looked up and spotted Henry standing there, his eyes wide in disbelief.

"Excuse please," said the plump nurse, in a thick Russian accent. "I don't see you standin'k there. How I'm helpin'k you?"

Henry was struck momentarily dumb. He opened his mouth then closed it again, not knowing what to say. The nurse smiled pleasantly. She picked up her clipboard and glanced at it.

"Ah, but you must be Henry Peppermint Tvist!"

"Yes," said Henry, timidly, wanting desperately to run away.

"Ve been expectin'k you," said the nurse standing. She threw a pink cardigan that matched her plump face over her wide shoulders,

"I am Grambera Jovanovich, but dees peoples calls me nurse." She laughed heartily, slapping Henry hard on the back, causing him to stumble forward a few steps. They walked down a long corridor with stark, white walls, their shoes squeaking beneath them on the highly polished floors. A moment later they were standing in front of a door.

"Room t've lve. It has a very nice view."

She opened the door allowing Henry to enter first. *"It was a pleasant little room,"* Henry thought. It was small and painted white, with a full sized bed, a night table, lamp and a chest of drawers to put his clothes in. A small desk sat along a wall next to the window. He also had, to his great relief, his very own private bathroom. *"It was like a hotel room,"* he thought, placing his suitcase on the bed and opening it to unpack. Nurse Jovanovich opened the curtains and window to let in the light and fresh air before she left.

"I puts clean towels in the bathroom, and ders a vending machine down the hall with toothpaste and such thinkgs should you be to runnin'k out. Dinner is at 6 o'clock, sharp! There is a list of activities on your night table and a copy of the menu." She opened the door. "I just know you are goin'k to love it here, Mr. Tvist." She smiled closing the door behind her.

Opening his satchel, Henry unpacked, then lay on his bed for a long time trying to erase his unpleasant thoughts. Old! It was a word he wasn't familiar with. Henry had never chronicled his age. In truth he felt no different than he had felt when he was a boy. His imagination was proof of that. The more he thought about it, the more tired he became, and the more tired he became, the more depressed he became. When he'd had enough of his own thoughts, he rolled over and waited, waited for sleep to come.

Henry awoke a few hours later, a bit disoriented, but otherwise fine. It took him a few moments to realise where he was. He got out of bed and readied himself for dinner. Several elderly people with trays were already in line when he arrived in the dining room a few minutes later. A sign by the serving station read: <u>Today's special: Roasted Chicken, Dressing, Mashed Potatoes, Stringed Beans, and Apfel Strudel</u>

"Did I oversleep, or is it the holidays already?" he asked aloud to no one in particular. A tall elderly man standing in front of him chuckled. He looked to be Henry's age.

"When you get to be my age, young fella, every day is a holiday!" he said, winking.

They both chuckled heartily. It was the first time in a long time for Henry, that he'd had a good laugh.

"For a minute there I thought I was Rip Van Winkle," said Henry, following the old man to an empty table and tucking right into his dinner. He was ravenous, not having eaten since breakfast that morning.

"I've been there a few times myself. Ben's the name, and you're Henry Peppermint Twist."

Henry looked surprised.

"Yes, but how did you ...?"

"Everyone knows the great Henry Peppermint Twist, chef de pâtisserie de maître," interrupted Ben in perfect French.

Henry blushed as he shook Ben's hand.

"How long have you been here, Ben?"

"Too long," Ben grunted, wrinkling his nose as he buttered himself a roll, "but to be precise, about fifteen years." Ben had a scruffy sort of voice, a bit gravely and deep. His face was less lined than Henry's, and his eyes were very clear and bright.

"You've been here fifteen years?" Henry exclaimed. "What brought you here, if you don't mind me asking?"

"No, I don't mind. What brings any of us here?"

"Old age?" replied Henry.

Ben's frown deepened.

"No indeed! Do you honestly think we would build places like this firetrap for ourselves? Certainly not! I have a house of my own, or rather, I <u>had</u> a house of my own."

His frown softened a bit. "The youth of today build these little camps so they don't have to worry after us when we get old." Ben took a mouthful of mash potatoes then continued. "I could never understand how one parent is able to care for several children and yet several children are unable to care for one parent in their golden years. Maybe I've lived too long." He took another mouthful of food.

"Just how old are you?" asked Henry, tentatively. He did not want to pry, but Ben fascinated him.

"One hundred and two," said Ben matter of factly, as he poured more gravy over his chicken and mashed potatoes.

Henry's fork made a loud clanking noise as it fell to his plate. "You can't be," he said in disbelief.

"And why not," Ben asked, raising his left eye brow.

"It's just … well, you look so young."

"Thank you for the compliment," Ben smiled, "but I really am one hundred and two. I wish someone would tell me what the heck one hundred and two is supposed to look like. Better yet, I don't want to know."

"What's your secret?" asked Henry eagerly.

"You really want to know?" Ben queried, leaning forward in his chair, so as not to be overheard.

"Yes!" exclaimed Henry, leaning in closer so as not to miss a word.

"First, you must understand that time is an illusion. Time is irrelevant; it does not exist. And second, and this is very important, the concept of age is a result of time. Always remember that you are only as old as you think and feel!" Ben smiled and leaned back in his chair.

"That's what they all say," said Henry, leaning back in his seat and sounding a little disappointed.

"No!" barked Ben, his face very serious, "that's the way it is!"

CHAPTER FOUR

Strange Little Men

The last of the summer days past quietly away, leaving autumn to seize hold of the landscape; turning everything it touched into red and gold. Cooler temperatures, followed by several days of rain, kept the residents of the Countryside Retirement Home indoors and wrapped tightly in their thick, heavy blankets, or huddled around the lounge's exiguous fireplace. Even with the soft glow from the firelight and three lit lamps, Henry thought this had to be the most dismal room in the entire building. Raggedy curtains, dust laden and careworn, hung at the four windows, which were also thick with grime and severely limited any natural light from entering in.

Five tables, with four chairs around each, made up the majority of furniture in this room. A small colour television sat in a corner surrounded by a very lumpy brown sofa and two mismatched chairs. A battered old upright piano, heavy with more dust and frothy cob webs between its legs stood in the farthest corner in desperate need of tuning. Henry spent very little time in the lounge, entering it only whenever he and Ben played chess. Most of his days were spent languishing alone in his room with only his unpleasant thoughts for company.

As the weeks rolled on Henry began to slip into deeper modes of depression. His face looked even more lined than ever before and his hair had become more silver. It wasn't until late November that things began to change.

Just two days before his sixty-seventh birthday something very strange happened to drive out all thoughts from his mind. Peering out of his bedroom window, which overlooked the back garden, Henry saw seven little men dressed brightly in all the rainbow colours move swiftly from the snow covered maze and into the forest. They wore funny little hats and had long white beards. They looked as if they had stepped from a page of a Brothers Grimm Faerie Tale.

One of the little men stopped abruptly, turned, and waved merrily up at him. Henry found himself waving back absentmindedly. He rubbed his eyes, wanting to make sure this was not an optical illusion, but the little man had vanished. In his place scampered a snowy white rabbit. *"Has the little man transformed himself? Impossible,"* Henry thought, not to sound ridiculous.

Several days later as Henry stared out of his bedroom window, the same thing happened. There he was again, that same little man in brightly coloured clothes staring up at him. He waved. Henry waved back. Henry pressed his nose against the glass, hoping to catch a better glimpse. There suddenly came a knock at his bedroom door and Henry's eyes turned to the door. Quickly looking back, he found that the little man vanished again. This time a deer disappeared into the woods. Was he having hallucinations?

"Come in," said Henry, perplexed.

"You have a visitor, Mr. Tvist," said nurse Jovanovich, poking her head just inside the door. "He is waitin'k in the lobby."

"What?"

"You have a visitor."

"Oh … yes, thank you."

"Is everything okay, Mr. Tvist?" Nurse Jovanovich asked.

"Yes, I just saw … never mind. I'll be right out."

Reaching the lobby moments later, Henry heard a familiar voice that made him forget all about the little man or his own troubles.

"I've been looking all over for you," said Wally, excitedly. "Are you all right? Are they treating you okay? Should I bust you out of here?"

"Hello Wally," Henry smiled. The muscles in his face felt tight from lack of use. "How did you find me?"

"Katie told me where you were. It's been tough getting to see her though. Brackmeyer makes it difficult for her to get away most days. He's been making her eat lunch at her desk. The only time I get to see her is when I walk her home after work." Wally blushed. He bent over quickly and opened his backpack. "I have something for you," He said pulling out a very large envelope and handing it to Henry. "Happy Birthday!"

"What's this?" asked Henry, pulling out a set of documents bound together.

"It's a business plan. I thought we could start our own sweet shop."

"Twist Treats?" said Henry, reading the cover of the business plan.

"Has a bit of a ring to it, don't you think?" said Wally, smiling. "I went to the library and borrowed all the books I could find on starting a business. Dad helped. The original will go to the bank when we're ready."

Henry perused the documents marveling at the amount of effort Wally had put into it. But his smile quickly faltered as he remembered his time at the factory, and considered his present situation.

"What's wrong?" asked Wally, noticing Henry's long face.

"I'm too old. Well, that's what they say at least." He gestured to the outside world. "After a while you start to believe it. Who wants an old pastry chef anyway?"

"So you've given up then? You admit yourself to an old-age home because Brackmeyer Sweets made you retire? You should have started your own sweet shop years ago. With your brilliance you could have put Brackmeyer Sweets out of business. Still could, if you were up to it."

The fire of excitement, usually found in youth, burned brightly in Wally's caramel eyes. Henry gave a weak smile and remembered, if only for moment, his own youth, and the feeling that he could do just about anything. Maybe Wally was right. What could it hurt him to give it a try?

The rest of November passed much better for Henry. All he could think about was the new sweet shop. Wally visited him again to talk about 'Twist Treats.' He also brought the latest gossip about Brackmeyer Sweets. Henry sat very still as Wally filled him in on the latest events.

"He's gone mad," said Wally throwing a nasty look up at the portrait of the man himself. "Since you left, the factory has gone quickly to the dogs. There have been a lot of changes."

"What sort of changes?" Henry asked, frowning.

"Machines," said Wally, darkly. "Brackmeyer fired half the staff and replaced them all with machines. You'd never recognise the place."

"But he can't do that!" Henry replied, outraged over the total disregard for human labor.

"He already has. Pretty soon there will be nobody left, humans that is. Mind you, I'm still lucky to be working there myself. Dad's been let go, though. That's why he's had time to bring me here and help me with the plans for the new shop. He's been on a few interviews in the area."

Henry's frown deepened. Never could he have imagined that Brackmeyer Sweets could ever treat their employees in such a manner. But this wasn't the Brackmeyer Sweets he knew. The old factory had disappeared, just like its founder.

"I want your opinion about something," said Henry, now digging into his pocket, traces of a frown still creasing his forehead. He handed Wally a piece of paper.

"What is it?"

"It's an idea I had for a new product. I call it Virtual Candy."

"What does it do?"

Henry's eyes now began to twinkle, as they always did whenever he was working on a new project. "Imagine being told that you could no longer eat sweets, due to an allergy or ailment."

Wally looked horrified. "I think I would rather have my head cut off."

Henry chuckled.

"Some definitely feel that way. For many, there is no other choice. But with this little device you can virtually eat any sweet you want without suffering the side effects or lack of taste."

"That's brilliant! Wally exclaimed.

Henry found himself still thinking about Wally's visit as his bedtime approached. He decided to take a walk, thinking it would help him relax. New snow covered the area. The air was cold and the evening sky quite clear. The moon hung like an opaque glass orb, full and round in the winter night sky. Henry imagined himself reaching up and nudging it from its place, but as he entered the maze faint whispers clearly emanated from a large hedgerow. One of the voices he recognised at once. It belonged to Ben.

Henry peered quietly around the corner so as not to be seen. The other voice belonged to that funny little man Henry had seen from his bedroom window. In his hand the little figure held a little glass ball that lit up the grounds all about them. Henry kept himself hidden behind the hedge and watched as Ben shook hands with the little man and proceeded to follow him out of the maze toward the dark forest. Without thinking, Henry quickly followed, entering the forest with nothing but the moon to light his way. Henry could see the two men up ahead and the tiny spec of light that was the orb shining brightly through the dense trees like a firefly. All too soon the thick canopy above blocked out the moonlight casting Henry into complete darkness.

Fifty yards ahead he could see the glow of the little light as it cut through the blackness like a light saber. Henry quickened his pace, keeping his eyes on that slice of light. Then, without warning, the little spec of light disappeared and Henry was again in complete darkness. He fumbled through the thick foliage his eyes pressed hard against the blackness, intent on reaching the two men. Suddenly a bright light, the brightest Henry had ever seen, erupted in front of him. Hurriedly Henry pushed forward, shielding his eyes. Then in an instant the bright light had gone.

Now he was in a clearing, and the moon was in full view again, bathing the ground he stood upon in pale white light. Squinting, Henry turned around. Where was Ben and that peculiar little man?

A gigantic boulder stood directly in front of him. It was at least ten feet tall with a very smooth surface. Large Pine trees grew all lumped together like some weird living fence on either side. Going around it was not possible, and climbing over it would be next to impossible without the right equipment. Two faint sets of footprints led to the base of the rock where they stopped abruptly. A strange idea entered Henry's brain as a soft breeze rumbled his hair, *"Maybe they passed through it,"* he thought. Henry touched the rock face and found that it was very solid. He pushed on it; when that didn't work he knocked. He didn't actually think that would work, but it was worth a try.

"Ridiculous," he mused aloud as he walked back through the forest, his head swimming with a lot of questions that needed answers.

Snow was falling in earnest as, a half an hour later, Henry made his way back to his bedroom. By morning there would be no evidence of his or anyone's trek into the forest, the snow would see to that. Maybe by morning he would awake to find his trip into the forest, chasing after Ben and some funny little man, had been some wild and far out dream.

As he had predicted, a fresh film of white covered every square inch of the grounds, wiping out all evidence of previous night wanderings. The police were combining the area hoping to find who Henry now knew they were looking for. Ben hadn't turned up for breakfast. Nor was he in his room when the nurse brought around his morning medication. The police questioned everyone about Ben's disappearance. Henry thought he should tell the officer what he knew and saw, but decided against it as it would look strange, and at the very least, suspicious. Who would ever believe that a three-foot-tall man dressed in funny clothes led an old man away into the forest on a cold November night? Henry retreated back to his room. He felt guilty for not revealing himself, and bitter disappointment for his lack of action

The next morning a small crowd had gathered around a bulletin board to read the new notice to residents from the police.

"From now on, there will be no more nightly walks near or through the forest! All residents must be indoors before sunset. Police will be patrolling the area after hours. Anyone caught out after dark will be fined. This curfew has been put in place to ensure your safety."

Chief Inspector, Jan Löhr

Mid-December brought a ton of snow, and extremely bitter winds blew in a few extra surprises. The rest home was a bit quieter after the incident. Many families were extremely intent on moving their loved ones home or to another facility. Wally visited every weekend leading up to the holidays.

"Brackmeyer is in a terrible rage at the moment," said Wally, punching the lumps out of his couch pillow.

"Is he now?" said Henry, not in the least surprised at the news.

"Yup, it's all those disappearances. He was talking about chaining everyone to their beds at night. I doubt that will happen, but Katie said Brackmeyer may be forced to close down the home."

Now there was something else to worry about. Where would he and the few that remained go if they shut the place down? It became more urgent now that he and Wally get things going on the Sweet Shop. If it was successful, he could buy a place of his very own.

Henry pondered this as he took a stroll through the maze that afternoon. It was a clear day. The sun shone brightly, making the snow on the ground blindingly brighter. He was just rounding a corner when he heard a slight commotion. Following the sound he wove his way through the puzzle of hedges, stopping just short of where the sound was the loudest.

Henry poked his head far enough around so as not to be seen. There, caught by the waistcoat and dangling from a very large hedge branch, was the peculiar little man.

"Let me go!" cried the little man. He had a squeaky little voice, like a mouse. "Let me go, let me go, you big dumb bush!"

Henry chuckled silently as the little man struggled to extricate himself. His feet dangled in midair as he kicked and flailed. But the more he thrashed about, the more entangled he became, much like a fly caught in a spiders-web. Unable to contain himself, Henry fell over with silent giggles. The little man caught sight of him and stopped struggling.

"Well, are you just going to stand there laughing? Help me down!"

Henry, still chuckling, rushed forward to untangle the little man.

"Don't you people ever trim these things?" the little man shouted grumpily.

Henry stood mute, not believing his own eyes. The little man brushed himself off and straightened his funny little hat, which sat crooked upon his head. He was an odd looking person with steely gray eyes, and a long white beard that matched the white snow covering the ground and touched the tips of his pointy toed shoes. He looked like one of those plastic gnomes that people put in their gardens for luck.

27

"What's the matter? Cat got your tongue?" he quipped, eying Henry.

Henry remained silent. When the little man had finished straightening himself up he moved closer to Henry and extended his hand in friendship.

"Henry Peppermint Twist," he said smiling, "we finally meet at last! We've waited an awful long time for you!"

"We?" said Henry, finding his voice at last and looking around the maze. "You mean there are more of you?"

"Loads," said the strange little man.

"Are you an elf?" he asked, hoping not to sound too crass.

The little man nodded and bowed very low. "Mackulian Winkleplixzen, at your service, but you can call me Mac."

"What do you mean; you were waiting for me? Why are you here?" asked Henry.

The little man smiled. "As for the first, we have waited for your arrival for many years, and as for the second, I've come for you!"

CHAPTER FIVE

The Other Forrest

"This is bizarre," Henry thought to himself as he stood awestruck, his mouth open at the elf's pronouncement.

"What do you mean you've come for me?"

The little elf again eyed him shrewdly. "What if I could take you some place where you could work without the fear of being fired? Would that be of interest to you?"

Henry chewed nervously on his bottom lip and scratched the back of his head as he thought. "It would," he said watching the little man curiously, "but no such place exists. Does it?"

"Ah!" said Mac, with a twinkle in his small gray eyes. "There is such a place." He moved closer to Henry. "And what if I told you that once there you would never grow old, what would you say to that?"

Henry looked at the little man incredulously. "I would have to say that you are either out of your mind entirely, or that you are suffering from the worst case of Peter Pan Syndrome I have ever seen."

The little elf scrunched up his nose looking very disgruntled. He pulled out a red and white stick from an inside pocket of his waistcoat. Henry winced, thinking he was about to receive a whack with it for his snide remark. Then he saw that the stick resembled a large piece of peppermint and that it had five holes in it. The elf put his lips to the tip of the peppermint flute and blew four notes. At once a door in one of the hedges magically sprang open.

"You have been here way too long, Henry. You have forgotten yourself. No matter, you'll remember soon enough."

The little man walked through the open hedge, slipping the flute back inside his pocket. He turned to Henry, who was standing there with his mouth open again.

"Coming?" asked Mac.

Henry hesitated for a moment, wondering if he should follow or not. But he needed to know. Besides, this would be his chance to learn what really happened to Ben and the others. He followed the little man out onto the open grounds and into the forest. Henry looked back to see the hedge door magically close, leaving no trace that it was ever there. They traversed deeper into the forest, following the same path Henry had been on that night he had followed Ben.

"Where are we going?" asked Henry, practically running to keep up with the elf.

"You'll see, and do try and keep up!"

They were soon in the clearing where the enormous boulder stood flanked on both sides by the weird barricade of trees. Once again Mac reached into his inside pocket and pulled out the red and white striped flute. "Stand back," Mac warned. He put the flute to his lips and blew the same funny little four notes. The rock began to shift and a crack appeared in the middle revealing a very bright light. The light began to seep through and with a loud crunch the boulder split wide open. A blinding array of multicolours poured forth from within. It was so bright that Henry had to shield his eyes.

"Come on, Henry," came Mac's voice from inside the cave.

Henry moved forward, still covering his eyes as the entrance to the cave closed behind him. It took a few seconds for his eyes to adjust to the brightness, but when they did, he couldn't believe what he was seeing. The entire cave, from floor to ceiling, was filled with the most precious stones Henry had ever laid his eyes on. There were blood-red rubies, dark green emeralds, and blue, yellow, purple, and orange sapphires strewn across the cave floor and embedded in the walls. Large stalagmites and stalactites glistened like luminous fangs in the same colours from the floor to the ceiling.

"There must be a fortune in here," Henry said, picking up one of the larger stones and examining it more closely. If he could gather up as many as he could, he would be able to pay for the sweet shop. Something of Henry's thoughts must have shown on his face.

"Try one," said Mac, smiling, and to Henry's astonishment, Mac popped a small red stone into his mouth. "Go on, Henry, they're not real jewels. They're candy!"

"What?" Henry gasped.

"Candy," Mac repeated.

Henry picked up a small blue stone and popped it into his mouth. It was the most wonderful thing he had ever tasted: a combination of blueberry and plum.

"What is this place?" he asked, sucking on the small stone, which seemed to get even sweeter and more flavorful as he sucked on it.

"This is the main chamber of the Rock Candy Mines," said Mac, his arms gesturing around him.

Henry looked around. Several tunnels branched off the main entrance in different directions.

"Every tunnel leads to a different cave. Every cave is of a different colour. Each rock has its own unique flavor."

Henry followed Mac out of the main cave and into one of the tunnels to the left of him.

"You'll want to be careful here," warned Mac taking out the orb light, "some of the tunnels go down as far as twenty-thousand feet. One wrong step…" he drew his finger across his throat.

"This is amazing!" said Henry, trying to take everything in.

"Oh, you haven't seen anything yet, but we mustn't dawdle!"

They traveled down the winding tunnel for what seemed like an hour, stopping every now and then so that Mac could point out a new flavored rock they had just discovered, or to introduce Henry to some of the cave-dwelling dwarfs that mined the stones.

The Dwarfs had long gray beards and long muscular arms that were attached to squat little bodies. In spite of their small stature Henry thought they looked incredibly strong. Each dwarf wore a tunic that matched the colour rock candy that they were mining. Henry was impressed at the skill and swiftness in which the dwarfs worked. He also noticed too that the pick axes they used had red and white striped handles, just like Mac's flute.

They hiked on, turning this way and that. It was like traveling in a rabbit's warren. Then there came a light at the end of the tunnel signaling the end of their journey. Henry began to feel a bit dizzy as he moved closer to the light. He stopped a moment to rest on a large orange rock.

"We're not far now, Henry," said Mac, who was positively bubbling with excitement. Henry gathered himself together and pressed on.

The light was growing steadily brighter. Henry's stomach fluttered. He had this strange feeling something was just not right. The light was at its brightest now as they approached the caves exit. Mac exited the cave, dancing and twirling about. Henry hesitated. Reason had finally caught up with him. What was he getting himself into? For a brief moment the thought of turning back popped into his head. But somewhere, in the canyons of his mind, was the urge to move forward, to find out what lay beyond. Giving in to his curiosity, Henry shielded his eyes once more. He held his breath, stepped out of the cave and into the light.

Henry opened his eyes. He was back in the forest. Only something was different. It was not like any forest Henry had seen before or had ever been in. Great red and white striped trees, as tall as redwoods, replaced the tall dark pines of the previous forest. A light dusting of snow covered the ground and there was a strong smell of mint in the air.

"Wow!" Henry mouthed, as he moved in for a closer look.

"This," said Mac, watching Henry closely, "is the Peppermint Forest."

Henry allowed his hand to touch one of the trunks of a tree as he examined it much closer.

"This can't be a Peppermint forest," said Henry, not believing his own eyes.

"And why not?" said the elf, incredulously, "have you ever seen a peppermint forest before?"

"N-no, but …" Henry stammered.

"Well then, how can you know for sure that it can't be a peppermint forest, if you have never seen one?"

Henry stared dumbfounded at the crafty little elf.

"Go on then, have a lick, and see for yourself if you don't believe me."

Henry stuck out his tongue and touched the tip to one of the large trunks. "Geez-Louise!" he cried, jumping back a few feet. "It *is* a peppermint tree!"

"I told you so," said the elf. "You're in a bonafide peppermint forest. One of the last I'm afraid." His smile faded a bit and a distant look of someone who has a lot on his mind took its place.

It was at this time that Henry noticed something different about his new little friend. Mac no longer resembled the elf he had first met. Mac had changed. Gone now was the snowy white beard, and his face was no longer wrinkled with age. A small boy, with pointed ears and that same mischievous smile stood before Henry now.

"You're young!" Henry shouted, rubbing his eyes, "but, how?"

"I've always looked like this, Henry. It was your perception of me that caused you to see me as you did. You think that all elves look like those you hear about in children's stories. So, that's what you saw. Things are not always what they appear to be, Henry. See for yourself."

Henry turned and faced a very large stone. What he saw made his heart skip several beats. There, reflected in a shiny, blue candy boulder was a boy no older than thirteen. Henry recognised the boy at once.

"This is impossible," he gasped.

"Nothing's impossible, Henry. Is it really so hard for you to believe?"

Henry didn't answer but continued to stare point blank at the reflected image of the boy. It was himself. He touched his own face and watched as the reflected person in the stone mimicked his every movement. He looked down at his hands. They were his, only younger.

"How ...? Henry began, but his attention was diverted as forty elves came marching toward them. Each wearing candy-striped overalls and carrying an ax.

"Zandlor!" shouted Mac, running toward the elf and embracing him like a brother. He motioned for Henry to join them. "Henry, this is Zandlor. He is the keeper and protector of the Peppermint Forest."

The elf grabbed Henry's hand and shook it vigorously.

"Welcome, welcome, Mr. Twist!" squeaked Zandlor, shaking Henry's hand and beaming up at him. "It's a pleasure to meet you at long last,"

"The pleasure's all mine, and please, call me Henry." Henry looked over their heads to several lumberjack elves all staring and pointing at him. They waved merrily at him, smiling, and chatting amongst themselves.

"Okay you lot," shouted Zandlor, "the shows over, back to work!"

Henry watched as each elf wielded his/her ax and began chopping at a tree. The blades were made out of colored rocks, sharpened and honed to a fine edge, then fastened to the end of a peppermint stick. The blades sliced through the tree trunks like butter. Soon the forest floor was littered with red and white striped logs. Henry was surprised to see that the tops of the trees were full of foliage; mint leaves. These too were harvested.

"What do you do with all the trees once you cut them down?" Henry asked.

"Well," said Zandlor, his chest expanding, "when a tree is felled it is taken over to the mill where we make all sorts of stuff: furniture, canes, flutes, and whistles, to name only a few."

Twenty elves quickly collected the fallen giants and removed them, one by one, from the site. A group came in behind them and began digging in the earth.

"What are they doing now?" asked Henry, curiously.

"Planting," said Zandlor. You must always give back to the land what you take from it. In a short time, these will be strong and healthy peppermint trees."

Sure enough tiny peppermint sticks were being planted in the holes the elves were digging. At that moment an odd ringing went off in Mac's pocket. He fished around inside his coat and pulled out a funny looking square object with lights. "Excuse me, Henry, Zandlor," said Mac, reading its funny beeps and flashing lights, "I must answer this. I'll only be a moment." He trotted off out of sight.

"Will you excuse me too, Henry? I've got to get back to work. Maybe later I can give you a tour of our mill."

"I'd like that," said Henry, smiling.

Zandlor trotted off, leaving Henry alone. Henry continued to watch the elves work. He found a nice sized boulder to sit upon while he waited for Mac to return. But as Henry sat, and sat, and sat, something very furry came scurrying around his feet. Henry jumped fully onto his rock, his legs tucked under him. There, pacing beneath him was the oddest looking creature Henry had ever seen. It had eyes as big and as round as saucers and big floppy ears like a rabbit. But it wasn't a rabbit, more like a dog.

Henry climbed down from the rock and cautiously approached the small animal, extending his hand slowly to allow the creature to grow accustomed to his scent. After the creature sniffed his hand, it gave Henry a small lick. Henry smiled and began to pet the creature. It closed its eyes lazily and purred. It even allowed Henry to pick it up after a while. When he did, however, the creature began sniffing the air and began to paw wildly at the inside of Henry's coat.

"Easy there fella," Henry pulled out a small bar of chocolate (one of his own, of course). "Is this what you want? I forgot I had this." The creature strained to get at the candy. "Okay, okay, hold on a minute," Henry chuckled as it licked his face excitedly. He broke off a small piece of chocolate and hand fed the dog-like rabbit.

What happened next happened in an instant. There was a small pop and right there on Henry's lap sat two creatures. Another pop and two became four then four became eight and so on. When Mac finally returned the forest was in a complete uproar. Henry was buried up to his neck in hundreds of fury little animals. Peppermint Lumberjacks were running around trying to gather up the scampering creatures as they dodged this way and that, avoiding their pursuers. Mac fell over with laughter.

"Don't just stand there laughing, said Henry wide eyed with shock, help me!"

Mac waded through the sea of fur and grabbed hold of Henry's hand and pulled with all his might.

"What are these things?" said Henry, in shock and disbelief. "One moment I was feeding it a bit of chocolate and the next ..."

"They're called Trifle's," said Mac, trying to contain his laughter. "They are native to Truffle Island. They have a very keen sense of smell for finding candy truffles, which grow underground. This one was brought back as a pet by one of the sailors for his children. He must have gotten free. Trifle's multiply when you feed them chocolate, Henry. But don't worry," he eyed Henry's long face. "It's not your fault. You wouldn't have known you're not supposed to feed a Trifle chocolate."

A large cage made out of peppermint stalks was being wheeled over in his direction. One by one the Trifle's were placed in it. The Trifle's shrieked and yelped, pawing at the cage to be set free. When the last of the Trifles had been caged the elves gave each other the high-five and sat for a moment, catching their breaths collectively and bragging a bit about how they had all cleverly caught their Trifle.

"What will happen to them?" asked Henry

"Grown rather fond of them already, have you?" Mac smiled. "These will be taken back to a farm on Truffle Island. We can't have them running around here multiplying. We'd be overrun."

Henry and Mac said goodbye to Zandlor and the rest of the Peppermint Lumberjacks a while later. Henry still looked a bit embarrassed and profusely apologised for feeding the Trifle.

"Don't worry about it," said Zandlor, waving away Henry's apology, "no harm done. Best bit of fun we've had in a long while."

They shook hands and He and Mac followed a red stone path that took them far away from the lumberjack encampment.

CHAPTER SIX

The Sweet Lands

Henry continued to follow Mac through the Peppermint Forest for what seemed to be several minutes. Mac was still laughing. "The look on your face when I came back," he giggled. He stopped laughing, however, the moment they reached the edge of the forest. Once more Mac's eyes twinkled with excitement. Henry stood very still, his mouth open in awe.

It looked very much like his beloved city from where he stood, with a few minor additions to the landscape. Before him were lush green fields and rolling hills as far as the eye could see. Splashes of colorful rocks were sprinkled all around and a vast array of flowers canvassed the ground. Henry noticed that they were standing in a field of what looked like golden hay. Giant rolls, set a foot apart, stood bundled together in staggered, but neat, rolls. To Henry's left, surrounded by what looked like a swampland, stood the largest structure he had seen in this strange but wonderful place. It was a mountain, snowcapped, majestic and completely made out of Chocolate. He could smell it from where he stood. Henry followed Mac down the sloping meadow and moved along a peppermint-log fence where several elves were picking things off trees and placing them into big woven baskets. Upon closer inspection Henry saw that several baskets held fruit while others held gummi bears, candy red and

38

caramel apples. His stomach grumbled noisily as he eyed the baskets. He continued to follow Mac along the red stone path that led directly to a village below. Three other roads, each a different color, marked a different route. With his eyes, Henry followed the blue path, which took the traveler north towards the mountains. The white path headed south towards the sea, while the yellow path, the shortest of the four, disappeared over a hill heading east.

"What is this place?" Henry asked, awestruck.

"Welcome to the Sweet Lands!" said Mac.

They moved forward into the open meadow where Henry got a closer look at things. Blossoms grew next to violets, roses, tulips and buttercups and other neatly arranged flowers. Mushrooms, some big enough to sit on, also dotted the landscape in small rings.

"WOW!" exclaimed Henry, bending over to sniff one of the roses.

"They're candy," said Mac, taking a moment to pop a small meringue mushroom into his mouth, "try one, they're quite delicious."

Henry plucked one of the petals from a buttercup and ate it, relishing the delicate, and sweet- buttery flavor before it dissolved into nothingness on his tongue. Several clumps of small bushes Henry couldn't identify grew wildly at his feet, their large plump, purple berries glistening between their shiny dark green leaves. On other bushes, smaller red berries were just beginning to turn.

"Oozleberries," said Mac, smacking his lips as Henry approached the bush for a closer look. "There never was a finer drink than wine made from Oozleberries!"

"I've never heard of Oozleberry Wine or an Oozleberry for that matter," said Henry, kneeling down to examine the plump purple berries.

"Then you are in for a treat," Mac winked. "Oh, and while we're here there's something I want to show you Henry, before we move on."

39

They moved off the red path and followed the yellow path over the hill which led to a spot thick with vegetation. Mac stuck out his hand and drew back the leafy green curtain to reveal an enchantingly secluded garden made up of a dozen or more trees. They entered. Hundreds of flickering lights twinkled through the leaves touching each of the tiny buds that were in bloom. Henry could hear a soft buzzing sound and for a moment he pictured bees gathering pollen. Soon the air was filled with tiny balls of light. Henry watched as it moved in a swarm onto the next tree where it came to rest, illuminating the tree in purplish-blue light.

A tiny ball of light separated itself from the others and moved swiftly toward them. Henry could just make out a tiny body and wings beating fiercely to keep it aloft. Then Henry realised that what he heard weren't bees at all, but faeries. It came extremely close to Henry's face tinkling angrily, which he surprisingly understood.

"Go away! You're not supposed to be here," said the little faerie, waving an admonitory finger, "they are not ready!!!" She flew off again to join the others.

Faeries…" said Henry, dreamily.

"Sugarplum Faeries," said Mac, matter-of-factly, "They inhabit this garden and care for the sugarplum trees. They don't care for visitors much, that's why they're hidden away. Soon the plums will be ready to pick. That's a job for Meara and her daughter Lalifin. They have a very special relationship with these faeries and are the only ones they will let near the trees."

They left the faeries in peace and got back onto the red path, passing several bubblegum bushes and gummi bear trees along the way. They soon came upon a lake filled with what looked like pink water. A sign staked into the ground read: **Pink Lemonade Lake. Absolutely No Swimming!**

Two elves in a rowboat were lying lazily about in it. Fishing poles made out of peppermint sticks were resting against either side of the little craft, and a line had been cast as if to catch something. Henry stopped to watch as one of the fishing poles gave a sharp tug. As quick as a thought one of the little elves sprang to life and began to reel in his catch.

Up from the murky depths of the lake came a beautiful red fish, but it wasn't a fish Henry had ever seen. Its whole body was red. It had a gummy look to it. Then the other pole gave a tug and the other elf sprang to life to reel in his catch. This time a yellow fish was brought to the surface. It too was solid in color with a creamy transparency. Henry gasped.

"Pastellfiskar, Henry," replied Mac, reading Henry's amazement.

"What?"

"Pastel fish, more commonly known by humans as Swedish Fish. We breed them here. When they get bigger we fish them out"

"What are they using for bait?" asked Henry, intrigued.

"Gummi-worms, of course," Mac replied.

And indeed Henry watched as the elves placed the fish in a large bucket and began placing gummi-worms on their lines. The multi-coloured worms wiggled and squirmed as they dangled on each hook and were tossed into the lake. This was certainly the most bizarre place Henry had ever seen. They continued on, passing by yet another orchard where on several trees grew large clusters of small reddish-brown pods. Several elves were already in the trees collecting the pods and dropping them in the waiting nets below.

"This is our test orchard, Henry," Mac explained. "These are Cacao trees. We wanted to see if we could get them to grow here."

"And you've succeeded," said Henry, happy to see something familiar. He had, after all, worked with cacao before, turning its seeds or 'beans' into chocolate.

"Not really," said Mac. "We are finding that the trees need a much warmer climate. We've tried everything to make them grow bigger pods. Heat lamps, canopies, you name it. They are best grown on the isle of Coca-Mocha. With these pods we make cocoa butter to use as a base for our chocolates and balms for our lips and skin."

Further on, Henry could see the mountains more clearly as they stood defiantly against the powder blue sky. Clouds as thick as cotton candy hid most of the summit from view. Henry gazed in wonderment; he had never seen one so big this close before.

"The Bittersweet Mountains," said Mac in a hushed voice, and for once he wasn't smiling. "We never go there. Well, not anymore."

"Why not?" asked Henry.

"Anise! She's a hag that lives there. Horrible creature. She has a taste for elf flesh." Mac shivered slightly in a momentary silence. "We haven't seen nor heard from her in a long while. Not since she put that spell on the swamp. You'd be wise to stay away from there altogether."

The village was now in sight, just over a small hill.

"We're here!" Mac cried, forgetting all about Anise the hag and pointing forward. He reached into his coat pocket, took out his peppermint flute, and began to play.

Henry took one last look at the mountain. He hoped he'd never had to meet this hag. "Wait for me!" he shouted after Mac. He had to run every few steps to keep pace with the elf, who was skipping, prancing, spinning, and twirling wildly; very much like a child who has eaten way too much sugar. The stone path they walked on became much wider as they entered the village. Small houses with even roof lines sat neatly in little rows, which put in his mind the thought of his beloved Apfeldorf.

The difference, however, were the houses. They all seemed to be covered in an assortment of candy: gumdrops, lollipops, cookies, marzipan and other candies, decorating the frosted roofs. As Henry walked through the village a pungent aroma peppered his nostrils. The smell brought back memories of the Christmas holidays spent in the kitchen with his mother and grandmother baking.

"Lebkuchen Haus," said Henry, dreamily.

And indeed it was, for every home was completely made out of gingerbread, and resembled a child's playhouse. The windows for each cookie house was made out of poured sugar, which was colored and elegantly designed to resemble stained glass. It was a sight that would have made even Hansel and Gretel eyes a little bigger than their bellies. There came a great shout of cheer as they approached the center of the village. Everyone had come out to greet them. Henry found himself being pulled to an oversized peppermint table by two female elves. Henry's stomach roared loudly with hunger as his eyes quickly scanned the bounty spread out before him. Roasted potatoes, carrots, and turnips sat in large glass tureens. Several bowls of fresh fruits and nuts were placed in various spots along the table. Freshly baked breads were piled high in woven baskets made from baked dough. Individual pots of honey and cakes of freshly churned butter sat at each place setting. There were also several pitchers of fresh cow's milk and many bottles of the Oozleberry wine Mac had spoken of.

Henry seated himself next to Mac, who had already started pouring a generous measure of wine into both of their goblets. This gave him time to examine the dinnerware more closely. They were the finest he had ever seen. The plates appeared to be made out of frosted glass with very detailed etchings of the solar system set around the edge, and in the center was a picture of the sun. The bowls, pitchers, goblets, and tureens were also made of glass, and had the same etchings as the plates. When everyone was seated and all of the goblets were filled with Oozleberry wine, Mac stood up.

"A toast," he shouted to the table at large, raising his goblet high in the air, "to Henry Peppermint Twist!"

"To Henry Peppermint Twist," they all echoed.

Henry tipped the cup to his lips and drank. He had never tasted such a wine. It tasted a lot like Elderberry, only sweeter, and a bit spicier than human wine. But very much like wine; for it made him feel very warm and very much at ease.

It is a fact, known to many humans who have studied faerie-lore, that when a person happens into the faerie kingdom they should refrain from certain activities; such as eating or drinking. To do either would render the person lost in the land of faerie forever. This fact, either by hunger or diversion, had somehow slipped Henry's mind. All eyes were transfixed as they watched him drink deeply.

"This is wonderful," said Henry, his eyes closed as he ran his tongue along his lips.

"Then have another," said Mac, refilling both his and Henry's goblets.

Henry loaded his plate with a little of everything. Ravenously he tucked in to his meal while an elf named Minkle played a delightful tune on his violin.

"That violin," said Mac, through a mouthful of roasted turnip, "was given to Minkle by a French faerie named Saule."

They ate, drank and laughed all through the meal as Henry listened to stories of elfin adventures, most of them in the human world. A short time later, when all of the plates were empty, Mac nudged Henry, who was feeling quite at peace with the whole universe.

"And now for my favorite part of the meal," said Mac, lifting his plate to his mouth, "dessert!" And to Henry's great surprise Mac took an enormous bite out of it.

Speechless, Henry watched as each elf picked up his or her glass plate in turn and began taking huge bites.

"Is there something wrong with your plate?" came a soft voice from over his shoulder. Henry turned to see a very beautiful elf with red hair standing behind him. But was she an elf? She had all the characteristics of one: her pointed ears for a start were a dead giveaway, and those eyes, azure green and mischievous. Henry found himself taken in by them, wondering what faerie secrets they held, and hoping he'd get the chance to discover them all. She was, however, considerably taller than the others. In fact, she was the same height as Henry and looked to be about twelve or thirteen. But something told him that she was a lot older than she looked. Maybe it was the way she held herself somehow, or the way she looked at him, with those knowing eyes. He couldn't put his finger on it.

"N-no," Henry stammered, starry eyed, coming out of his wistful daydream.

"Henry," said Mac, swallowing a piece of plate, "this is Emlin, daughter of Dram and Nimiah."

Emlin took hold of Henry's hand and shook it firmly. Henry stood speechless, staring into her eyes and watching as a small section of her hair fell softly over one side of her face covering her left eye.

"Pleased to meet you," said Henry at last. His stomach did a couple of somersaults. He felt nervous -- she was very beautiful.

"The plates are edible," she said in that soft melodious voice. "Try it. You'll find it quite tasty."

Henry broke off a small piece of his plate and put it in his mouth. The very mellow sweet felt smooth and silky on his tongue, like butter, with just a whisper of mint.

"It's wonderful," he said, breaking off another piece and popping it quickly into his mouth.

The Celebration was in full swing now. Henry couldn't remember when he had a better time. He and Emlin had hit it off rather nicely. She refreshed his goblet of Oozleberry wine just as Minkle played another jig on his violin. Full of wine, Henry was unable to contain himself. He grabbed hold of Emlin's hand and led her into the center of the dancing frenzy. The music lasted well into the night. Henry was dragged into the ring by many of the elfin females as they all danced around him.

Emlin was sitting at the table talking with Mac. Both looked up as Henry approached. Mac yawned and stretched broadly. Elves lay scattered about, wine sodden, their goblets still gripped between their fingers. Others were starting to make their way back to their homes now.

"Henry, Emlin will show you where you'll be staying. I'll see you in the morning." He bounded off, whistling one of Minkle's tunes.

"I'm not sleepy," Emlin proclaimed.

"Neither am I," said Henry.

"Let's walk a bit."

"Okay."

They walked around the village in silence for a few moments. Henry kept glancing over in Emlin's direction. He noticed a slight grin had appeared in the corners of her delicate mouth.

"I know what you are about to ask me," she said, not looking at Henry.

Henry smiled nervously, could she read minds too?

"You want to know if I am an elf."

She can read minds, Henry thought.

"I wasn't born here," She said, recalling a time long past. "My parents died when I was very young. I was sent to an orphanage not too far from the rest home where you lived. When I was five, I wandered off into the forest and got lost."

"You must have been very scared?" said Henry, hanging on to her every word.

"No," said Emlin, "Somehow I wasn't. I was found hours later, they tell me. Dram found me fast asleep in a faerie ring. He brought me here to live with him and his wife Nimiah. They became my parents and taught me the ways of faerie."

"That's a great story," said Henry. They continued to walk all around the village until finally Henry yawned, the wonderful food, the Oozleberry wine, the fun and diversion, and the walk around the village were all starting to have a soporific effect on him. "I feel I can sleep for a week."

"Then I will show you where you will be staying," said Emlin.

Henry followed Emlin to an odd little vehicle that resembled a golf cart and a steamroller. A big basket of Lemon drops hung on the dashboard in between the driver and passenger seats. An equally large funnel, attached to a long hose, sat above that.

"Hop in, Henry," said Emlin, climbing in herself and fastened her seat belt. She reached in the basket for a lemon drop and popped it into her mouth. As she sucked the sour candy, Henry's glands watered and his lips puckered. A few seconds later, she spat into the funnel. The cart took off with a jerky start. "Feel free to help," she cried, gesturing to the basket and spitting furiously into her funnel, "the more we spit, the faster and longer we'll go."

Henry picked up a lemon drop and popped it into his mouth. Immediately his glands began to overflow with an abundance of saliva. He spat into the funnel and once again the cart jerked speedily forward. He and Emlin spat like crazy as the little vehicle sped along a lengthy path through the village. A short while later, after both lemon drops had dissolved, Emlin applied the brakes bringing the cart to a full and shuddering stop.

"We're here," she said, unbuckling her seat belt and climbing out.

Henry remained in the cart, massaging his jaw, a bit bewildered. Looking around him he noticed that they had gone in a complete circle around the village ending up in the exact same spot they had started.

"That was fun," said Emlin, beaming. "Your house is two over from the left. We'll walk from here."

"I'm sorry, but weren't we just here?" Henry asked, trying desperately not to sound rude.

"Yup!" said Emlin, her green eyes twinkling.

"Couldn't we have walked?"

"I suppose we could have, but what would be the fun in that?"

For a split second, Henry saw just how very much like an elf Emlin really was, for mischief danced in her eyes. They walked silently for a time. All of the houses sat in neat little rows enclosed by a fence made out of cinnamon sticks. Beautiful beds of edible candy flowers filled the yards. *" I'm Home,"* he thought. It felt like some weird dream he was having, only he was awake. They presently came upon a gingerbread structure the size of a child's playhouse.

"I don't mean to sound ungrateful, but how on earth am I going to fit in that?"

"Nothing is as it seems, Henry." She grinned, turned, and pushed open the door to reveal a quite normal-sized room inside; normal, that is, for humans. They entered through the three-foot tall door as if by magic.

"Whoa!" said Henry in breathless wonderment.

Several oil paintings hung on the walls behind ornate gold leaf frames. The canvases and frames were all made of tempered chocolate. The gold leaf that decorated the frames was edible too. Even the various colors used to paint on the white chocolate canvases were made of powdered food-coloring mixed with melted cocoa butter. This gave Henry the illusion that the artist used some sort of oil-based paint. All about the living room were beautiful handmade furniture, direct, Henry gathered, from the Peppermint Lumberjack Mill. A bevy of potted edible plants, flowers and shrubs seemed to take up every available space.

"This is the living room, Henry."

"Yes," said Henry, looking around at the small rain forest growing in the front room, "very nice!"

They traveled down a short hall to another room. Henry found that this door was closed, and for good reason. When he had opened it and entered, he was immediately swept off his feet by a pair of mechanical arms, which stripped him of his clothes and carried him away into a tidal wave of water and soapsuds. Three scrub brushes, washcloths, and towels were moving about at different stations. It was like a car wash gone mad. Henry was scrubbed and rubbed, tossed and spun until every square inch of him was clean, dry and smelled of cocoa. When he appeared out at the other end the expression on his face was like one who has seen some sort of horror. He was dressed, however, in a brightly colored bathrobe, matching pajamas and slippers. Emlin greeted him with a very large grin on her face.

"Wasn't that fun?"

"Yeah, I like the part where I nearly drowned," said Henry sarcastically.

Emlin led him to another closed door. Behind it Henry didn't find hundreds of plants, or a room full of soapsuds. What he found was a room completely filled with water, at least 6 feet deep, like a large indoor swimming pool. A wooden pier wound its way around the walls, where floating aimlessly in the middle, a large bed was neatly made. It had sheets of woven corn silk and a colorful comforter made from pressed leaves all sewn together.

"Okay," said a very confused Henry, "living room I got-- plants and such. The bathroom okay, But what is with all the water in the bedroom?"

"It's a waterbed," said Emlin clapping her hands and grinning broadly, "And look!" she said pointing toward the ceiling, which revealed a beautiful star strewn sky. "Your ceiling reflects what is happening outside. Do you like it?"

Henry could tell by the look of anticipation on Emlin's face, that she had had a hand in creating this room for him.

"Yes, I do."

Emlin beamed. As bizarre as everything was, he had to admit, all he had seen today was all very cool. Later, Henry sat in a large chair by the fire place in his living room, drinking a cup of hot chocolate Emlin had made. It was the richest he had ever tasted in his life. Like the Oozleberry wine the hot chocolate seemed to relax every square inch of his body, making him forget for the moment that he very nearly drowned. He took a second to reflect back on his life growing up. This house, his bedroom, as crazy as it may seem to most, wasn't so in the eyes of a child. As a child, Henry often imagined himself floating along on his childhood bed, visiting fantastic and far-away places in his mind. He would have given anything to have a room like this one, secretly wishing he could stay young forever. But by some strange miracle, he *was* thirteen again, and his very wish had somehow come true fifty-four years later. He yawned, swallowed the last of his hot chocolate, and went off to bed.

Henry waited on the tiny pier not knowing how he was to get into bed. Was he expected to swim out to it? As he stood thinking about sleep, his bed slowly drifted over to him as if summoned by his very thoughts. He climbed carefully aboard and got quickly under the covers. In spite of all the moisture in the room the sheets and comforter were quite warm and dry.

The moon was large and full in his ceiling's sky. He felt like he was outdoors on a boat. Henry lay for some time on his back, staring up at the ersatz sky, watching the stars twinkle and glimmer like diamonds. *"It had really been a strange, yet wonderful day,"* he thought. And as his bed drifted slowly back into the center of the room, Henry, warm and snug under his covers, fell fast asleep.

CHAPTER SEVEN

The New Factory

Henry awoke the next morning to a bright lemony yellow sun beaming down upon him from his ceiling. His bed, once again sensing what he wanted, drifted slowly towards the pier. When he had dressed he found an assortment of bread, jam, cold cuts, cheese and a pot of Emlin's delicious hot chocolate waiting for him on a small peppermint table in the kitchen, along with a note from Mac:

Henry, meet Emlin and me by the chocolate pond as soon as you are up and had your breakfast. Just follow the orange path. That will lead you to us.

-Mac

Henry left the small gingerbread house some time later, taking a few souvenirs for his trip back to his world, should he need proof that he was not having a grand hallucination. Henry followed a small orange path that led him down a long and winding trail lined with Bubble Gum bushes and Gummi-bear trees. He found Mac and Emlin moments later, skipping jawbreakers, large round hard candies, into a small brown pond. Henry walked over and began skipping jawbreakers with them.

"Good morning, Henry," said Mac, a mischievous smile playing around his mouth, "sleep well?"

"Like a newborn babe," Henry replied. "Boy, will I have a story to tell when I return."

Mac and Emlin looked at each other, their smiles fading a little. It didn't go unnoticed.

"What's the matter? Oh, I get it. I can never tell what I saw here, is that it? Don't worry your secret is safe with me."

Mac and Emlin's smile vanished entirely.

"What's the matter with you two this morning?" Henry pressed.

"Well you see, Henry, it's like this …," started Mac, avoiding Henry's eyes.

"You can never go back," Emlin blurted.

Henry froze, his eyes darting from Mac to Emlin

"What do you mean I can never go back?" then something in Henry's mind clicked into place. His eyes grew wide as the horror of Emlin's words sank in. "Oh, no!" he cried. All those faerie stories his grandmother once told him as a boy came flooding into his memory like a tidal wave. "You've tricked me!"

He dropped his pail of jawbreakers and ran in the direction of the Peppermint Forest. Mac and Emlin ran after him.

"Henry, wait … please, stop!"

Henry blocked out their yells and ran faster. He had been pixie-led. *"How could he have been so stupid?"* He thought. He reached the Peppermint Forest and weaved his way through the dense red and white striped trees, not knowing where he was exactly, or how far away he was from the cave. He kept running, determined to find the exit at any cost. And then, not knowing exactly how, he found it, the place where he and Mac had exited the cave.

Mac and Emlin were still a good distance behind him, calling for him to stop. With a quick glance behind him, Henry entered the cave, trying to recall the path he and Mac took through it; and recalling, not the way out, but an old story his grandmother once told him about a young man who was led away by the faeries.

There once was a young man who had been eighteen or nineteen years old, as the story goes, who returned home after listening to faerie music one afternoon. But upon coming home, he found that his parent's house had very much changed. Ivy grew unchecked along the front and sides of the house, something that his father had never neglected to keep under control, and the grass and weeds were high all around. An elderly gentleman, whom the young man had never seen before, was standing in the doorway. As the young man approached the elderly man asked the lad what he wanted, to which the young man replied:

"I have left my mother and father but minutes before in this very house."

"What is your name?" asked the elderly man, and when given it, he became deathly pale. "I've often heard my grandfather speak of your disappearance." At this pronouncement, the young man crumbled into dust before him on the doorstep.

Was this to be Henry's fate as well? Would he too turn to dust once he left the cave? Henry ran past several dwarfs in the tunnel. He could see the dazzling rainbow of the multi-coloured rocks dancing off the walls and ceiling up ahead of him. He reached the main cave and began searching the walls frantically for the secret doorway. Henry ran his hands along the wall until his fingers came across a slightly protruding rock. Upon pushing it, the entrance to the cave began to crack open. Henry could hear Emlin's frantic screams for him to turn back, to stop. He stood at the caves' opening for a brief second, not knowing what was to happen. He closed his eyes and stepped out into the sunlight, back into the human world.

He felt a little funny at first, a little light headed. Then his whole body started to tingle. He looked down at his hands, they were growing older by the second. He fell to his knees, his hands over his eyes. Things inside him were hardening and his body felt as if it were on fire. He fell forward, his head hitting the forest floor. Henry struggled to remain conscious. He saw several pairs of feet coming out of the cave running towards him.

"Henry, Henry," called the far away sounding voices around him as he was moved back inside cave. He had a brief moment's view of a pair of green eyes before everything went black. He had passed out.

When Henry regained consciousness he found that he was back in the Sweet Lands, adrift in his waterbed, with Emlin sponging his forehead. Henry's focus was blurred. His whole body was sore and stiff. On the pier, he made out the blurred image of Mac who paced back and forth.

"What happened?" asked Henry, hoarsely, his mind still very foggy.

"You almost died, that's what!" said Mac, his periwinkle eyes wide as saucers.

Henry tried to sit up, but his head throbbed. Emlin gently placed her hand on his shoulder, coaxing him to lay back.

"It's best if you rest a bit, Henry. You need to regain your strength," she said softly.

Emlin poured Henry a large goblet full of Oozleberry wine, which she mixed with a white powdery substance. It started to froth and hiss. Lifting his head slightly, she tipped a good measure down his throat. Warm sensations began to spread rapidly throughout his entire body. Once again he felt very relaxed, and in no time his focus had improved slightly. His head stopped throbbing as well.

"What did you put in the wine?"

"Dried bongo buds," said Emlin, tipping the goblet to his lips again.

Henry lay back on his pillow not feeling it necessary to ask what bongo buds were at the moment. His thoughts were becoming much clearer now. His attention shifted to his friend Wally, Twist Treats, and his own imprisonment in the Sweet Lands.

"What happened to me out there? I felt like I was going to die."

"And you <u>were</u> dying," said Emlin, in an anxious tone, her green eyes glistening with tears.

"What did you go and do a silly thing like that, for?" asked Mac, his brow furrowed. "You gave us all a fright!"

"Well, maybe I wouldn't have run out, if someone would have told me the truth to begin with!" Henry said, nettled.

Mac went silent, his frown wiped clean. "I never meant to hurt you, Henry," he said, his face elongated in sadness like a child being scolded by its mother.

"Oh, it's not your fault entirely, Mac," said Henry, his anger ebbing away. "I should have known better."

He attempted to sit up again. He only did so with Emlin's aid.

"But what I can't understand is what happened to me? I mean, one minute I was young, the next I was getting older. Why is it that you and the other elves can leave the Sweet Lands and I can't?"

Emlin pushed the goblet back to Henry's lips. The more he drank, the better he felt. He was able to move his arms and legs around a bit better now, and his vision was no longer fuzzy.

"Henry," said Emlin in her soothing voice, which made Henry feel like he had just drank another goblet full of Oozleberry wine, "we are not of your world. We are Fey. We live in a land of faerie-dreams and magic. In the Faerie-realm, time runs differently. We can go where we will and not be affected by time as you are, and once I was. The moment you came into the Sweet Lands and ate and drank with us, you left behind all of the rules that govern the human world. In our world time stands still."

Henry's mouth fell open. "You mean I am more than sixty-five years old?"

"Here you are ageless! As it should be, Henry. You have, somehow, tricked your brain into believing that you are ancient and useless when in your heart you know the real truth. It is that truth that allows you to see yourself as you are now."

"We had to get you away from that environment, Henry," said Mac, "before you really became old!"

Henry took a moment to let all of what he'd just heard sink in.

"What about my friend, Wally? We were going to open a Konditorei. We were going to call it Twist Treats."

Emlin looked over at Mac who was now sitting on the pier, his bare feet dangling in the water. He caught Emlin's eye, smiled and nodded as if he were reading her thoughts. Henry could see between them the sparkle of elfin merriment, mischief and magic dancing in their eyes.

"I think it's time we showed you something," said Emlin and there was a hint of a smile nestled in the corners of her mouth.

Henry, Mac, and Emlin stood in front of an enormous gingerbread structure a short time later. The Oozleberry wine laced with Bongo buds had done its job well; restoring Henry to perfect health. The structure he was now looking at was several times the size of all the other houses in the village. Thousands of cookies and candies decorated the façade. The windows were different too, clear instead of multi-coloured glass. The roof was also made of a different material. It was thatched, made from the same shredded cereal Henry was made to eat as a boy. A light dusting of icing sugar on top gave the appearance that a soft snow had fallen in the night. Once again Henry was reminded of the Brothers Grimm tale of Hansel and Gretel.

"Who lives here, a witch?"

"No," Mac chuckled. "You've been reading too many children's stories. This is the Sweet Lands Factory."

They entered. The place was an explosion of movement and clatter. Hundreds of elves were busy at work. At least fifty elves worked diligently, making, boxing, and wrapping all kinds of wonderful treats. This put Henry in mind of the infamous workshop in the North Pole where Father Christmas and his elves made toys for deserving little girls and boys. Over at a large marble table sat several elves working with white and dark chocolate and turning it into all sorts of wondrous edibles. At another table, several elves were busy frosting cakes. On a conveyor behind that, five elves sat in a row filling cooked pie shells with fruit or cream fillings.

Henry was led straight away to an office, catching glimpses of elves pulling taffy, caramelizing sugar or melting chocolate. He reached a large door with his name embossed in big black letters. Too excited to speak, Henry stepped inside and at once he felt he had been here before. This office was exactly like his old one at Brackmeyer Sweets. From Henry's desk, right down to the many mini cauldrons, test tubes, and colorful liquid-filled beakers. The room was recreated with strict attention to detail. About a half a dozen elves busied themselves in this room, each working on something different.

"Like it?" Emlin asked, tentatively.

"It's wonderful!" he managed, his eyes over bright.

Emlin and Mac beamed.

On an easel across the room sat a set of blue prints. A small piece of white paper with a crude drawing was pinned to it. Henry approached for a closer look. Upon closer inspection he realized at once what he was looking at.

"My plans!" said Henry, rushing over to them. "How on earth did you find them?"

And indeed they were his plans for his Virtual Candy device.

"It took some doing, I don't mind telling you!" said Mac, sitting on a nearby stool. "It wasn't easy breaking into that retirement home once they posted guards all around it."

"Guards?" said Henry, inquisitively. "Why are there guards around the retirement home?"

"There were guards. They were looking for you, of course," said Mac, looking guiltily at Henry.

"We think your friend Wally called the police after you disappeared," said Emlin, also looking a bit guilty. "But you've been gone now for many years. They've finally closed the place down."

Henry ran his hand over his face and through his already disheveled hair. "I've just got to find a way to reach Wally. At least get word to him that I'm okay."

"Perhaps I can help," said an unfamiliar voice from behind him. Henry wheeled around. An elf in a long white lab coat and large goggles came forward, his hand outstretched. He had a very serious face, with deep, rich violet eyes, and wild black hair that stood up like it had been electrified.

"Ah, Henry," said Mac, hopping off his stool, "this is Gobo. He's the factory's chief engineer and gadget maker."

Henry shook hands with the little elf.

"Pleased to meet you at last," said Gobo the elf.

"Likewise," said Henry.

"Let me show you what we've been working on in your absence. I think you will be quite pleased with what you're about to see." Gobo walked over to a table where a small box sat. He opened it and took out something that was small, square, and red.

"What is it?" Henry asked, turning over the odd little gadget in his hands.

"I call this a Candy Com," said Gobo. "You can communicate great distances with this little beauty. It runs on eighteen volts of sugar power. Tested it myself yesterday just outside the tunnel, and as far as the factory. It worked fine. You will have no problems communicating with your friend."

"That's fantastic!" Henry said, turning it over and eying it more closely. "What are the two lights for on top?"

"The green one means it's fully charged," Gobo said, pointing to the large green light. "The orange one is a warning that you have two days reserve left. I suggest that you charge up as soon as the warning light comes on."

No words could express Henry's gratitude. He shook Gobo's hand vigorously and showered him with thank-you's. Now he could talk to Wally without having to leave the Sweet Lands. Gobo drew Henry's attention away to what looked like a pair of high tech laser glasses.

"Try these on," Gobo said, handing them to Henry and leading him over to sit in a chair. "You'll find we've made a few modifications to your original plans."

The old drawing of his Virtual Candy Device was an awkward-looking contraption, large and bulky, resembling a biker's helmet with large goggles. Several little multi-coloured wires stuck out all over the place. What Henry held in his hands were very light and thin and the size of a normal pair of reading glasses. He put them on while Gobo made a few adjustment; checking to see that they fit snugly around his head. When he had finished, Gobo pushed a small button on the visor's left side. Almost at once, Henry got a visual of an ordinary bar of chocolate.

"I'd thought we'd start with the basic candy bar then work our way up. Try and reach for it, Henry."

Henry reached out his hands into the blank space in front of him. A pair of virtual hands came into view reaching toward the candy. Henry closed his hands. His virtual hands mimicked his, wrapping around the bar of chocolate. Henry pulled his empty, real hands back toward his mouth. It was a strange feeling to watch a pair of virtual hands move as if they were his own. Once the virtual chocolate was in range of his mouth, he took an imaginary bite. He felt the creamy, rich milk chocolate swirl around on his tongue. Gobo and the other elves watched silently, each looking intensely at Henry as he chewed and swallowed. Then a smile spread across his face.

"Delicious! That was the best imaginary chocolate I've ever tasted!" he exclaimed, as the room exploded in cheers and applause.

Henry sent an elf that day to deliver the Candy Com to Wally, along with a note:

Dear Wally,

Meet me in the forest near the rest home at 4pm. Follow the path until you arrive at the base of an extremely large rock. You can't miss it. I'll explain everything to you then. Bring this box with you.

Your friend,
Henry.

CHAPTER EIGHT

The Meeting

The next day Henry waited just inside the entrance of the cave. As long as he stayed just within threshold he would be safe. He paced nervously back and forth, a million thoughts tumbling through his mind like candy sprinkles. Most prominent of these thoughts was the time difference between the two worlds. Would Wally remember him after all this time? Would he even be alive? The answer to that came as the noise of crunching leaves and snapping twigs made its way closer to the entrance. A young boy, who looked to be no more than eight or nine years of age, came bouncing into the clearing. He was followed closely by a young girl, who looked to be the same age. She was holding the hand of a much older man.

Henry watched as the man and two children approached the cave. Pulling a handkerchief out of his back pocket to wipe his brow the man took a seat on a nearby stump next to the entrance.

Henry studied the man's face more closely. "This couldn't be Wally," he thought to himself, his brow furrowed. Then he remembered Emlin's words: "In the Faerie-realm, time runs differently!" Could this really be his friend Wally? He found the answer in the man's eyes. They were the same caramelizing brown color as Wally's, though hidden behind a thicker pair of spectacles. Recognizing his friend at last, Henry smiled.

"Hello, Wally," he said warmly, as six pairs of eyes rested on him.

"Hello," Wally replied, looking around somewhat confused, "I was told to meet my friend, Henry, at this location."

"It's me, Wally, I'm Henry!"

"You're not Henry Peppermint Twist," Wally said incredulously. "Henry would be much older, by now. Much, much older in fact." He scratched his head, now more confused than ever.

"But it *is* me, Wally," said Henry. "I can prove it." And he launched into the story of what happened after their last meeting. About his encounter with an elf named Mac, and how he was pixie-led to a place called the Sweet Lands. After he'd finished, Wally sat with his mouth agape.

"I know it all sounds a bit wild," Henry began, "but I really am Henry."

Wally thought a moment. "What was the last thing we talked about before you disappeared?" he asked.

"We were going to open a shop of our own. We were going to call it: Twist Treats."

"It really *is* you!" Wally exclaimed, nearly falling off his stump. "But you've been gone a long time! How did you get to be so young?"

"That, my friend, is a long story. But tell me first, who are these two children with you?"

"Oh, forgive me, Henry, these are my children, Heinrich and Gretchen, they're twins, though not identical. Children say hello to the famous Henry P. Twist. The finest master pastry chef that Apfeldorf has ever had."

"Hello!" muttered the children, not really knowing what to make of all of this.

The children, Henry suspected, must have resembled more of their mother for they looked nothing like Wally. They had sandy blonde hair, and pale blue eyes.

"Hello," replied Henry. He launched into an explanation of what had happened to him; and, as best he could, all that Emlin had explained.

"So now you know the whole story," he said, finishing at last. He allowed them a few minutes to get used to the information.

"You mean there are such things as faeries?" asked Gretchen, dreamily, breaking the silence.

"Yup!" replied Henry smiling.

"Awesome!" exclaimed Heinrich, punching the air with his fist. He too was captivated by the tale. "Then there will be dwarves, Trolls, ogres, dragons and all kinds of mythical creatures too, right?"

"I haven't seen any trolls, ogres or even dragons yet, Heinrich, thank goodness. But I can tell you that there are dwarves working deep in this cave behind me."

Henry smiled as he saw the children's faces light up with excitement. This was the fire of youth that had seemed to be extinguished in him over the years. This simple, raw belief that children have in the world. The enthusiasm was infectious. It made him feel warm inside and more like himself again, ageless, and useful. He turned to Wally, trying to contain enough of his own excitement, as the children prattled on about the Faerie kingdom.

"Wally, do you still have those plans for the sweet shop?" asked Henry.

"Yes, Henry, why?"

"Because I was wondering if you were still interested in opening Twist Treats?"

"Interested?" said Wally, jumping to his feet; the shocked expression vanishing in an instant. "It's all I've been thinking about for years. "I'd do anything to get away from Brackmeyer Sweets."

"Still at the factory?" Henry asked raising an eyebrow. "How is old Brackmeyer doing these days?"

"Worse!" Wally replied, crinkling his nose as if he just smelled something rotten. "After you disappeared they shut the retirement home down. Brackmeyer went nuts. He fired even more people and replaced them with machines. We've got a skeleton crew of about one hundred to work them, a far cry from the four thousand the factory used to have." He shook his head.

"What about Katie? Is she still with the company? Think she would help us?"

Wally grinned sheepishly. "She might."

"Where is she now? Did something happen between you two?"

"I'll say it has," said Wally ready to burst.

Henry eyed the two children, identical in looks, chattering away behind their father.

"Wait a moment. You and Katie?" Henry looked into his friend's eyes.

"Yeah!" Wally grinned, sheepishly, and he launched into the details of their long courtship, and how Katie would sneak out of the house at night to meet up with him; and how he had proposed to her after college.

"I bet old Brackmeyer didn't like that one bit," said Henry, chuckling.

"No, he didn't," said Wally. "And when we had children, he threatened to disinherit her."

"What did Brackmeyer do?"

"Well Brackmeyer couldn't do anything. It seems that once Katie turned 18 she was to receive her share of her grandparents' estate, which also included that of her parents. He tried to keep that from her too. Lucky for Katie, her grandfather left her inheritance in other hands. We are quite well off, money wise.

"But you still work at the factory?" asked Henry.

"Well, yeah, I am pretty good with computers. Besides, part of Katie's inheritance is half of the factory. Brackmeyer wants to keep us close; hoping that he can buy her out. She keeps turning him down. Katie says she wishes the factory would close. No one buys the pastries there anymore. The people really miss your sweets, Henry."

"Then maybe it's time they taste them again. He tossed Wally a key, which he caught deftly in his right hand. "Take this key to the bank, I have a safety deposit box there. In it you will find my Will and other documents making you my heir if anything ever happened to me. You were the closest thing to a grandson to me. I should still have a fair bit of money left in my account. With the interest over the years we should have enough to open our own business."

Wally looked a bit overwhelmed. A tear trickled down his left cheek, which he brushed away quickly. Henry acted as if he didn't notice.

"But how are we ever going to start a business with you there and me out here?" Wally said, concernedly.

Henry smiled. "Well, that's the best bit. Did you bring the box?"

Wally reached into a bag by his feet to pick it up, "Got it right here."

"It's a Candy Com. Use this if you need to reach me. You should be able to talk to aliens from another galaxy with the kind of power that thing runs on. Should you come into any problems just contact me. Oh, and if ever the orange light flashes, call me immediately. It will need recharging."

Wally examined the funny-looking device as he took it out of the box, turning it over and over in his hands. "I still don't understand how this is all going to work," he scratched his head, looking more confounded as ever. "What's even more difficult is how I am going to explain this to Katie."

CHAPTER NINE

Twist Treats

Henry and Wally met every week, laying the final plans for Twist Treats.

"As for the sweets, Wally, meet us here with a van and the elves and I shall fill it up with whatever it is you are out of. Just give us a call on the Candy Com. Oh, and speaking of places, have you found a location yet?" asked Henry.

"Way ahead of you, Henry," Wally replied, pulling out a bunch of photographs of potential buildings. He handed them to Henry.

Henry thumbed through them slowly, trying to envision what he had always thought his own sweet shop would look like. His gaze finally came to rest on a set of photos of an old apothecary with very big windows. Snap shots of the interior revealed large cherry-wood counters and lots of shelving.

"This one," said Henry, handing a set of photos to Wally.

"I knew you'd liked this one," Wally replied, grinning from ear to ear. "It was the first one we looked at. Gretchen found it. She really has an eye for detail. Needs a little work though, but it has everything we're looking for, except the sweets."

"Not to worry," said Henry, taking out a small bag and tossing it to him. "Let me know what you think of these. It's my latest creation."

Wally popped a small truffle-like piece of candy into his mouth. He closed his eyes as he chewed it slowly, savoring the creamy dark chocolate. Henry could see Wally's caramel eyes widen, signaling to him that he had gotten to the candy's center.

"Whoa, that was wonderful!" he said, dreamily. "What do you call them?"

"Cocoa-mint Surprise," said Henry, beaming. "A Coco-truffle creation with a creamy mint gel in the center."

"They'll go bonkers for these," said Wally, his face still carrying a faraway look.

"Just wait till you see what I have lined up for the kiddies," said Henry, positively bursting with excitable energy.

"I can't wait. Old Brackmeyer will be on the unemployment line in no time," chuckled Wally.

"Speaking of Brackmeyer, how did Katie take the news?"

"Well," said Wally, "I don't mind telling you that she was ready to have me committed. But when I showed her copies of your Will and the other documents, and the children backed my story up, she believed me. She is going to help us."

"Good!" said Henry, "let's get to work."

Everything was going according to plan. Wally, Katie, Heinrich and Gretchen worked hard to get the new shop ready to receive sweets. By late September, Twist Treats was ready to open its doors. Wally and Katie had given up their jobs at the factory; a move Henry knew would anger Brackmeyer. The children had also pitched in. Every day after school, including a few hours on Saturday, they cleaned counters, swept the floors and stocked the shelves. On Sunday morning, the day before the grand opening, Wally and Heinrich visited Henry at the cave entrance in the forest. Hundreds of boxes awaited transport to the shop. Elves loaded them into the back of Wally's van while two elves, cleverly disguised, would make the trip back with them to help get things ready for the next day.

"I'll send back photos," said Wally climbing into the van.

Opening Day arrived with much fanfare. A marching band played outside as long lines cued up and extended for a whole block. Inside, Heinrich and Gretchen were busy wiping down the beautifully restored cherry-wood shelves and counters. Gumdrops, licorice whips, jellybeans, chewy caramels, rock candy and sheets of candy buttons filled many glass jars that rested on the polished countertops. Along one shelf was an assortment of candy bars Henry had invented especially for Twist Treats. There were Mellow Mallow Bars: **for over-active children, and their parents,** an idea that Gretchen had come up with after babysitting a pair of hyper-active four year olds. The strange Will O' the Wisps Bars: an elusive vanilla-flavored sweet that seemed to disappear as soon as you popped it into your mouth, leaving no trace whatsoever that you had ever eaten one. And lastly, Goodie Cookie Bars: **for naughty children.**

Each of these candy bars were individually wrapped with gold foil and pastel paper with the name **Twist Treats** written in block lettering. A small silhouette of Henry was artistically placed in the center of each wrapper. Gummi Bears ranging in size from one to nine inches sat wrapped in cellophane on a shelf opposite. Also on a shelf were Tangulicious Taffies: chewy sweets you could stretch for miles before gobbling them up, and Coffee Toffees: small candies that felt as if you were drinking a hot cup of coffee. These were wrapped in different colours marked with the words 'Black,' or 'Cream and Sugar.' On another shelf were small lollipop trees to plant in your garden, and next to that, flowers made out of pulled sugar that really grew.

Two refrigerated glass display cases were filled with trays overflowing with the most succulent sweets one could ever imagine. Fluffy éclairs and delicate napoleons were each filled to bursting with Bavarian cream, flavored with either rum or Grand Marnier. On a shelf below that sat several decadent cakes, pies and fruit tarts. The second display case was filled with all sorts of delicate candies enrobed in milk, white, or dark chocolate, each with a decorative swirled signature of what was lurking inside. There were great slabs of fudge in many flavors, mountains of truffles, peppermint creams, peppermint ice and Henry's own Cocoa-mint Surprise.

There were several barrels located in different areas around the shop filled to the brim with many novelty sweets such as giant Candy Canes: **For walking or eating.** Rainbow Lollies: lollipops that turned colors as you licked them. Ventrilo-Sweets: **suck them and you can throw your voice for blocks,** a nifty sweet created by Heinrich, who was a bit of a prankster. Super Bounce Bubble Gum: **bounce them off the walls and into your mouth**; great fun for when you were bored out of your skull.

On a counter behind the glass display sat a great brass machine. Wally stepped back after polishing it to admire his work.

"And you say your uncle was about the throw this away?" asked Wally, now addressing Katie, who was over at the display table.

"I know. Lucky I found it when I did. It was just sitting there collecting dust."

"Well, this little baby will make the best hot chocolate people have ever tasted," said Wally, beaming with pride.

On a shelf of its very own sat The Virtual Candy Visor. A small placard beside it read:

> *Do you suffer from sugar related ailments? Are your pants getting too tight? If you have answered yes to any of these questions then try a new, very safe and guilt free way of eating. Virtual Candy: the candy that's virtually free from reality!*

Within the first week of its grand opening, Twist Treats did a whopping big business. Great lines continued to form outside the shop. Wally and Katie managed to take on a few workers that had been let go from Brackmeyer Sweets. After some time, Henry and Wally felt Katie should see him and the elves.

They talked in great length of how they would do it. The best way, both agreed, was to bring her along on Wally's next trip into the forest for supplies. On the appointed day, Wally, Katie and the children stepped out of the van and walked over to the large boulder, the entrance to the hidden cave. Katie's mouth dropped upon seeing the giant rock split apart, revealing the boy who used to be an elderly man. Henry was standing there, a big smile on his face.

"Hello Wally, Heinrich, Gretchen. Hello Katie," he beamed at them.

"Hi Henry," said Wally, looking a bit nervous.

"Nice drive in?" asked Henry, making small talk.

"Not bad," Wally replied.

Katie remained stock still, unable to move, as the children rushed over to help the elves load the boxes into the van. A look of utter disbelief sat frozen on her face. It wasn't until an elf crossed her path that she moved at all. She had fainted straight away. Wally revived her, giving her a few moments to get used to the idea that faeries really did exist. Once the van was loaded up with new supplies, Wally and Katie and the children said goodbye to Henry and the elves. They all watched as the entrance to the cave closed, leaving no trace that there was anything odd about the large rock. Wally turned to Katie and the children.

"This will be the secret of Twist Treats. We must do everything we can to ensure that this secret remains with us and only with us, agreed?"

They all nodded their agreement.

"The last thing we need is trouble from dear Uncle Charles," finished Wally, as he turned and faced the steering wheel.

Though everyone agreed trouble was hard to avoid, especially when Brackmeyer Sweets, and its tyrant of an owner, were not far away. And right now neither one was doing very well.

CHAPTER TEN

The Return of Anise

In the coming weeks it was clear that Twist Treats had become everyone's favorite place to go to for their favorite sweets. Patrons, once loyal to Brackmeyer Sweets, now gave their allegiance to the fledgling little shop.

The drop in sales at the factory, however, hadn't gone unnoticed, even though Brackmeyer Sweets continued to produce the same volume it had done in the past. But by using machines and not people, the quality was poor and the taste suffered. Products were returned to the factory by the truckloads. But what was worse, at least for Brackmeyer, was that he had to give back every penny to all the companies that returned their orders. Soon, several companies who had done business with the factory for many years stopped carrying the sweets in their stores all together. By the time news of the tiny sweet shops success reached the ears of the president on the fourteenth floor, the factory had stopped all production.

Twist Treats continued to see an influx of new faces now standing in line. Though at first many grumbled about the extra ten minutes it took to get from Apfeldorf to the neighboring town of Usingen, it only took one bite of a buttery jam filled croissant, or a mouthwatering cream filled éclair, or one of

Henry's Cocoa-mint Surprises to make the ten minute drive a rather tasty inconvenience.

Everyone worked hard to keep the shop stocked full of sweets. But no one worked as hard as Henry. He seldom took breaks and almost always was the last one to leave the factory. Some nights he never left at all, working straight through the night and into the wee small hours of the morning. "That's when some of my best ideas hit me."

But Emlin did managed to convince Henry to get some rest by preparing him a sleeping draft made up of hot chocolate, dried bongo buds, and mint leaves.

"Get some rest," Emlin pressed, making sure that Henry drank the chocolaty potion. "We are going on a foraging expedition in the morning and I need you well rested for the walk."

They were up and out before sunrise and traveled over the lush green meadow of the Sweet Lands, stopping whenever they spotted a clump of wild ripe Oozleberries.

"Oozleberries are best picked at the peak of ripeness," Emlin explained.

By mid-day their baskets were filled to the brim with plump ripe berries.

"What's next on the list?" asked Henry plopping down on the grass to rest. They had been walking all morning.

"We are also running low on Bongo Buds," said Emlin. She gazed apprehensively toward the Bittersweet Mountains.

"Don't tell me," said Henry, cottoning on, "we have to go into the swamp to get them, right?"

"Not exactly, the buds grow along the border, not too far in. We should be fine," replied Emlin, sounding skeptical even by her own words.

Henry turned his gaze toward the Swamp and wondered what else lurked in the darkness that made the elves avoid going in unless they absolutely had to.

"Let's get going. I want to be back to the village before nightfall."

B. W. Van Alstyne

They walked in silence. Henry caught sideways glances over at Emlin who apparently was deep in thought. Meanwhile, the Bittersweet Mountains loomed ever closer, rising like some ancient titan from the earth below. They approached the entrance to Treacle Swamp and stopped a few hundred feet short of a well-worn path that seemed to lead directly, as far as Henry could tell, to the mountain. A great wall of darkness stretched from one end of the swamp to the other; its vastness as deep as it was wide.

"Shall we continue?" asked Emlin, her voice tremulous with fear.

"Yes," said Henry, trying to display courage he didn't quite have at the moment.

They entered. It was like walking into a black hole. All of the light was instantly extinguished, absorbed by the nothingness as they moved further inward. The darkness pressed hard against Henry's eyes as he strained to see two feet in front of him. Henry could feel what little confidence he had vanish like one of his sweets. He heard Emlin rummaging around for something as she walked blindly beside him. There was a *click* and suddenly light flooded the area around them. Henry looked at Emlin who was holding a small orb, exactly like the one Mac carried when he had followed him and Ben through the forest.

She held it high above her head so that the light lit every area of the forest it touched; brushing away the darkness like excess flour on a bread board. They worked quickly and silently, gathering up the Bongo Buds as they found them. Henry kept looking over his shoulder into the remaining darkness. He had the strangest feeling that they were being watched. Soon they had enough buds to last a good long time, remembering that time ran differently in the Sweet Lands than in the human world. Nevertheless, they felt they had plenty.

"Let's go," Emlin urged. "I'm feeling a bit synxt."

"If that means strange," said Henry, looking a bit puzzled, "then me too." He continued to glance over his shoulder.

They exited quickly and walked several yards before stopping. Henry placed his basket of Bongo Buds and Oozleberries beside a large white candy boulder and sat with his back against it. Another quick glance up at Emlin and he knew something was wrong. Emlin had not set her baskets down. She didn't sit down either. She just stood stock still, her eyes wide with fear. Henry quickly got to his feet.

"Emlin, what's wrong?"

Emlin didn't look at Henry. She didn't speak. She just stood there, pointing toward the swamp. Henry followed her finger as it guided his gaze upward into the Bittersweet Mountains. A light was emanating from one of the caves above where a shadowy figure stood in the entrance looking down upon them.

"C'mon, Henry," Emlin urged finding her voice. She turned on her heels and sprinted off. Henry tried to keep pace with her but kept falling behind. She was extremely fast. Emlin ran like a deer taking long strides and leaping over boulders with the least amount of effort. Henry supposed that her being part elf had a lot to do with it. They came upon Mac resting at his favorite spot, a large bubblegum bush, a candy-stone's throw from the chocolate pond.

"Back so soon?" Mac asked as he got to his feet.

"She's back, Mac," Emlin wheezed clutching a stitch in her side. "Anise is back!"

Mac's mouth dropped open. For a minute Henry thought the little elf had been struck dumb.

"Anise, back, are you sure?" He managed.

"Henry and I both saw the light in her cave and there was someone looking down at us. Who else could it have been?"

"We'll need to alert the Captain immediately," said Mac and without another word he sprinted off.

Henry and Emlin followed closely behind Mac as he moved quickly off the path leading to the village onto another that took them over a hill to where an encampment lay at the bottom of a small gully. Several brightly colored tents were scattered about like jelly beans along the ground below. An even larger multi-coloured tent was placed in the center.

Henry, Mac, and Emlin descended the hill and over a small peppermint bridge that led to the center of the encampment. Twenty elves, dressed in camouflage jumpers, were gathered together in a clearing where they stood in a line side by side. An elf dressed in a sapphire blue camouflage jumpsuit stood apart from the rest. Around his neck hung a small peppermint whistle, on which he gave two short blows. To Henry's bewilderment each of the elves sprang forward and executed a perfect cartwheel forming two ranks. The elf blew on the whistle again, this time two long bursts. Immediately both lines began to cartwheel inward in perfect synchronicity, crisscrossing within an inch of the other. Henry thought it remarkable that at that speed they never touched or broke rank.

"Looks like they've learned a few new combat moves," said Mac eying the cart- wheeling elves with pride.

"Combat moves?" said Henry, incredulously.

"Diversionary tactics," replied Mac, giving Henry a wink and laying a finger aside of his nose and tapping it twice, he ducked inside the large tent.

As Henry entered the tent his eyes fell at once on a humongous map that was spread out over a large peppermint table. Several elves were standing over it, plotting the best strategic course to take. An elf in a multicolored jumpsuit with matching hat looked up as Mac approached the table. Mac threw a funny little salute as he popped to attention. The elf returned the salute almost lazily, his attention on Henry.

"Henry, this is Captain Ogglebog," Mac dispensed quickly then immediately began relaying what the pair had seen while picking Bongo Buds in the treacle swamp. The Captain's complexion turned the color of vanilla ice cream.

Captain Ogglebog scratched his head under his hat. He had a faraway look in his eyes that gave Henry the feeling that things were not okay.

"Well, this just confirms our suspicions. Two of my scouts went missing two nights ago. There have been reports of a disturbance near the entrance of the swamp."

"A disturbance … that sure sounds like Anise" said Mac, wiping his sweaty forehead and taking a seat in a nearby chair.

"There's only one way to know for sure," Captain Ogglebog said gravely. "We'll have to send another scout to investigate."

The room went deadly silent. Henry looked into each elf's anguished face. It was clear that neither one of them would volunteer themselves willingly to visit the Bittersweet Mountains, let alone to verify that this Anise person was actually back. He was still somewhat confused as to who this person was.

"But who is this Anise?" Henry asked, breaking the silence and noticing that all eyes were on him now.

"She is a Swamp Hag, Henry," explained Captain Ogglebog. "Treacle Swamp wasn't always as dark as it is now. Ages ago the swamps were the domain of king Gloop and his treacle kin. For many ages we lived in peace, trading elfin-made goods for treacle. Then one day three sisters came to the Sweet Lands. And what horrible creatures they were, too. They had eyes as black licorice and hair to match. They chose to live in the caves carved out deep inside the Bittersweet Mountains by their long sharp fingernails. Vicious and evil though they each were, there was none more evil than Anise."

Everyone inside the tent, except Henry, gave a little shiver.

"Worst of the three, Anise had a voracious appetite for elfin flesh. Many elves lost their lives due to her nighttime prowls. An uncle of mine nearly got eaten by her once. He was on a climbing expedition in the mountains and came across the Hags lair. He barely made it out alive. He still wears the scars. He hasn't climbed since. He is a sailor now on a cargo ship called the Popillol."

"What happened to these hags?" Henry pressed.

"Two were destroyed entirely after that incident but Anise got away. Disappeared, but not before placing a curse over the entire swamp. The Treacle people were forced to live in small sticky ponds scattered throughout the dark swampland. We looked for her, but she had vanished. She was never heard from or seen again."

"Till now," said Henry, gravely.

Henry looked out of the tent at the elves and watched as they continued their flipping and somersaulting exercises. *"If truth be told,"* he thought privately to himself, *"a few acrobatic elves were no match for an evil and magical swamp hag."* He continued to watch the elves; wondering, as an afterthought, if things could get any worse.

Meanwhile, back in the human world, Charles Brackmeyer sat in his candle lit office on top the fourteenth floor seething with anger.

"Traitors!" He spat, glancing at an advertisement of Twist Treats in the paper.

He blamed Twist Treats for all of Brackmeyer's Sweets misfortunes. He flicked through his phone index until he found the name he was looking for. He picked up the phone and found that it too, like the lights, was no longer in service. Brackmeyer cursed, then slammed the receiver down hard on its cradle.

""They'll pay for this!" he screeched to the room at large.

CHAPTER ELEVEN

Brackmeyer Breaks Through

The fame that once belonged to Brackmeyer Sweets was no more. This fact, though wonderful news, wasn't taken very lightly. Henry knew that when it came to money the factory's president would use all of his resources to make sure he held on to what was his. This proved true in the coming days as Brackmeyer had hired a man to spy on Twist Treats. He was a heavy sort of man, with a big round belly, which made him look like he had just swallowed a large pumpkin. He wore a long, dark coat with several pockets for which he stored his camera and several different lenses. The man waited outside the shop, watching the Hingle's every movement. He took notes on when Wally and Katie arrived in the morning and what times they left. He also followed them around town, hoping to find the secrets to their success. After a week his stake outs paid off.

The family left the shop early Sunday morning to pick up a fresh supply of treats in the forest of Cratzenbach, unaware that they were being followed. When they reached the forest the man hid himself among a thick patch of trees. *Click-click, Click-click*, went the shutter of the man's camera.

"What was that?" Henry stopped to listen, "that clicking noise."

Wally, Katie and several elves all stopped loading boxes to listen.

"There it was again, that *Click-click, Click-click,* sound," said Henry, concernedly.

They looked frantically around, but it was Heinrich who spotted the man in the dark coat who lay nearly invisible among the trees and leaves that littered the forest floor. Having been spotted, the snooping man ran for it. Fear ripped through the group. If word ever got out about their little operation all would be lost.

"We've got to go after him and find out who he is," said Wally. He started to run after him, but Katie held him back.

"No need, Wally. He works for dear Uncle Charles, and besides, I am sure he will want to see us soon enough. I'm sure he already knows that we helped put the factory out of business."

"We need to finish loading the van," said Henry, urgently, "before anyone else discovers our little secret."

Hours later, back at Brackmeyer Sweets ...

"These photographs show me nothing!" snapped Brackmeyer, throwing the blurred images back onto his desk.

The photographs revealed Wally, Katie and the Children loading boxes into the van. Several blurred images appeared around what looked like boxes hovering in mid-air. It was hard to tell if they were being supported by something or someone.

"But they were there, sir, I swear. Little elves coming in and out of that cave in the forest. They helped load boxes into the van," said the Spy.

"Stop talking rubbish, man," there are no such thing as faeries!" Brackmeyer spat. "You say this forest is the one near the retirement home?"

The spy nodded.

"Interesting. I must go and see this place for myself. I am sure I'll find a more logical explanation for what you saw. Elves, indeed!" He turned his back on the man and looked down at the set of blurry photos. "But first I must have a little talk with my dear relatives."

Days later, Wally and Katie were back at the cave.

"So, Brackmeyer didn't say anything about me or the elves?" asked Henry, hopefully.

"No," said Katie, "and that's the strangest thing. The photographs that his spy took only caught us loading boxes into the van. I don't think Uncle Charles believed the man's story."

"He won't stop until he knows exactly what is going on," said Henry taking to pacing the cave floor. "We'll have to be on our guard from now on."

"Maybe if we stagger our pick-ups a bit. You know, never come at the same time?" Wally suggested.

"That's a good idea. Let's try that." said Henry.

And so they did. Wally and Katie changed the pick-up times for every delivery. They even took different routes to get to the forest. Henry couldn't shake the feeling of deepening doom. It felt like they were being surrounded on all fronts. With the return of Anise to seek revenge on the Sweet Lands and Brackmeyer's determination to put Twist Teats out of business, Henry's biggest worry was who would strike first. He got his answer on the next pick up day.

"Henry," Mac called out, huffing and puffing as he ran to meet him and Emlin at the path leading to the Peppermint Forest. "Brackmeyer's here and is heading this way!"

"What!" Henry looked over his shoulder in the direction of the Peppermint Forest.

"And that's not all," Mac's eyes widened, he looked even grimmer, "Wally has run in after him. Katie called on the Candy Com as soon as it happened."

"Oh no," Henry sighed, as he followed Mac and Emlin into the Peppermint Forest.

They found Wally standing directly in front of the cave looking scared and confused. Passing through the tunnel hadn't caused him to change.

"We heard the news," Henry announced as he, Emlin and Mac approached Wally. "What happened?"

"Brackmeyer met us as we were about to load up the van with supplies. He must have been camping out in the forest, waiting for us to return. When he saw the elves going into the cave he ran in after them. I didn't realise he was there until he had gone in"

"We've got to find him!" Henry urged,

At that precise moment something jumped out from behind a large candy boulder. That something was Brackmeyer. And he had changed. He was no longer the pale, thin man Henry had remembered. In fact, he wasn't a man at all. Brackmeyer had transformed into a very ugly, hairy ogre with powerful, short arms, pointed ears, and a long tail. The ogre Brackmeyer grabbed Wally from behind and held him in a tight headlock. Henry and Mac started forward.

"One more step and I'll break him in half!" roared the ogre.

"Let him go Brackmeyer!"

"And who are you to be giving orders? You are just a little pip-squeak!"

"I am Henry Peppermint Twist!" said Henry, almost as proudly as he did in Brackmeyer's office those many years ago when he was being fired.

"Twist?" said the ogre, squinting. "But you can't be, Twist is an old man. He'd be dead by now!"

"I am alive, no thanks to you and that shack you called a retirement home."

Brackmeyer's eyes narrowed. "So it's been you all along. You're the one that's been causing me all this grief. Well, no more!"

Soon many more elves had appeared trying to surround the ogre as Wally continued to struggle to free himself from Brackmeyer's unbreakable grip. But the ogre held on all the tighter. He began to drag Wally away, keeping his back to the open forest in the direction of the Bittersweet Mountains.

"If any of you try and follow, I will break him in two," yelled Brackmeyer from a distance. Then in one fell swoop, he picked Wally up and threw him over his shoulder like a sack of potatoes and carried him off.

"What are we going to do?" Emlin asked, "We just can't let Brackmeyer get away with this."

Henry thought for a moment. "We'll need a plan. I think it's time we called on the Gumdrop Patrol!"

CHAPTER TWELVE

Revenge

Henry, Mac, and Emlin huddled around the grand peppermint table inside Captain Ogglebog's tent. The captain was given all the information Henry knew about Brackmeyer.

"This is bad," sighed Captain Ogglebog, "very bad indeed. We all know what Anise is like alone, but if what you are saying about Brackmeyer is true and that he is heading for the Bittersweet Mountains, there is no telling what may happen if he should meet the swamp hag."

"We've got to try and rescue Wally. We can't just leave him up there." Henry got to his feet and began pacing. He tried to bully his brain into coming up with a clever idea to rescue his friend. Walking always helped him to think better.

"I agree," said Mac, "we cannot let Wally spend one minute more with that ogre, let alone Anise."

Captain Ogglebog went over to the tent flap, pulled it back, and called for an elf. A very spry, young elf, judging by the look of him, came bouncing in. He popped to attention and gave the captain a funny salute, which reminded Henry of a child's teasing game he would play in order to be chased. The captain returned the funny salute and introduced Henry to him.

"Henry, this is Linxz. He is one of the finest and bravest scouts we have. If anyone can find your friend, it's Linxz."

Henry and Linxz shook hands.

"Linxz was just about to do a bit of scouting up in the Bittersweet Mountains. Linxz, old man, I'm afraid the situation has taken a very bad turn. Henry's ex-boss has entered the Sweet Lands and has escaped with a human hostage to the mountains."

Henry noticed that the little elf was not disquieted by this sudden pronouncement. In fact he seemed positively eager, too eager, for Henry's liking.

"I'll get the packs ready, sir! Coming, Henry? I'll need you along to identify your friend," squeaked the little elf.

The sun was setting as Henry and Linxz made their way from the Gumdrop Patrol encampment and over the grassy fields and rolling hills of Sweet Lands. Before long they were standing at the entrance of the swamp. Cold chills seemed to race up and down Henry's spine.

"Hang on to this and stay close," said Linxz, handing Henry a piece of roped licorice that was tied to his waist. "Things get a bit tricky as we get further in."

Henry grabbed hold of the candy rope as he was instructed. He gave and involuntary shiver as they proceeded into the darkness.

Like before, the blackness pressed hard upon his eyes as they continued to travel deeper into the swamp. The darkness seemed endless, even with the little ball of light Linxz now held in his hand. For the most part he directed the light on the path at his feet. "Look at the lighted path, Henry, and step where I step."

They had been walking for what seemed like several minutes before Linxz threw out his arm to stop Henry. On the swamp floor, just a few steps in front of them lay a large pool of sticky brown goop. Linxz raise the ball of light to his face and put his finger to his lips and whispered,

"We will have to go around, but be very quiet. We don't want to wake anything up."

Henry nodded and Linxz lowered the ball to shine its light on the swamp floor, avoiding the bubbling pool. They picked up the path and quickly walked onward. They were met by several other such ponds of treacle every hundred or so feet. Henry took his eyes off the ball of light and looked straight away. His eyes were finally starting to see a glimmer of light up ahead.

"Almost through," Linxz whispered back.

As they exited the swamp, a faint glow could be seen high above them in one of the caves. Looking up, Henry took in the sheer massiveness of the chocolate mountain. He looked for a way in, but Linxz had other plans. Reaching into a sack he had flung around his back, he pulled out several long feet of black rope, just like the one he had held onto while going through the swamp, only longer. Attached to the end of the rope was a peppermint grappling hook. He swung the rope over his head and let it fly up the side of the mountain. Henry heard a soft thud and watched Linxz give a couple of strong tugs to make sure the line was secure.

"Okay then, up we go, Henry, you first," said Linxz, extending the rope to Henry.

"We're not going to climb, are we?" asked Henry, "can't we just go through there?" he pointed to the cave opening.

"This is the quickest way to get there without being seen," said the little elf. "It would take an awful long time to maneuver through all those caves. There are hundreds of them."

Henry didn't argue. No telling what kind of tortures Brackmeyer was putting Wally through. He grabbed the shiny black rope and started his ascent up the side of the chocolate mountain, catching faint whiffs of star anise coming from the black shoestring rope he was using. He dug his foot in hard as he climbed up, up, up, until at last he and Linxz were sitting on a narrow ledge just under a window-like opening of the lit cave.

Henry and Linxz peered inside. Wally was sitting, tied to a large brown stalagmite that jutted up from the chocolaty floor. Henry spied the ogre Brackmeyer lumbering in with handfuls of long black rope he was fashioning into a whip. Henry turned to Linxz. "We'll need a diversion so that one of us can free Wally," he whispered. Linxz nodded.

Henry looked back through the window, waiting for the right time to act. Then out of the shadows and into the cave emerged a horrible creature.

"Anise!" whispered Linxz.

It was true what they said about her, Henry thought. She was horrible to look at. Her eyes were as black as cauldrons, and far colder and crueler than even Brackmeyer's. Her hair was a long, tangled weave of black licorice that partially hid her hideous face, which was as pale as the Ice Cream Sea.

Henry watched as Brackmeyer spun around and faced her, hoping against all hope that a confrontation between the two would be just the distraction they needed to set Wally free.

"Who are you?" Henry heard the ogre grumble as he rushed over to the hag. "How did you get in here?"

"I could ask the same question of you," said the hag, in a soft, but deadly voice, "seeing that these caves belong to me!"

"I don't see your name on them," said the ogre smugly. "What do you want old woman, I haven't got time for idle chit chat."

The hag stood silent and motionless in her spot, her raven-colored eyes transfixed on the ogre. When she spoke again it was like a blast of cold arctic air, which made the sparse hairs on the back of Henry's neck stand on end.

"For several years I have waited, and it has come at last. What I want, sir," she said looking at Brackmeyer, "is to help you." She glided over to Brackmeyer as if on wheels.

"And why would you want to do that?" asked the ogre, looking suspiciously through squinted eyes.

"Revenge," said the hag in almost a whisper. "I want revenge on those miserable little elves that killed my two sisters! I want revenge for driving me away from my beloved home in the swamp." She sniveled, pretending to weep.

"I don't need any help, thank you very much!" said Brackmeyer, now turning his back on the hag and checking the ropes that bound Wally. "I have everything under control."

Anise stopped her pretend weeping at once. "Don't you now? And how, may I ask, do you plan on destroying their little candy making operation when you possess no weapons or even an army? Yes, I know all about your silly little plan."

Henry's stomach gave a jolt. So that's what Brackmeyer was up to. He wants to destroy the Sweet Lands factory. Anger now surged through his veins, replacing the fear almost at once. He was not going to let that happen. He and Linxz continued to listen.

Brackmeyer was looking stupidly at the hag who was moving even closer to him so that their faces were an inch apart.

"I can help you." She said, her sharp yellow teeth poking through her grin. "Hidden in one of these caves, known only to myself, is a machine capable of producing the very army you need in order for your plan to work."

Brackmeyer's thin lips curled in an evil smile. "Show me this machine at once," he demanded.

The old hag only turned her back on him and sat down on a nearby rock. "I will bring you to this machine under one condition."

Brackmeyer moved forward. "Get on with it." He said with the same impatient tones Henry was accustomed to hearing.

Anise continued. "Give to me the elves to do with as I please." Her black eyes flickered maliciously and Henry thought he saw the hint of her green tongue move slowly across her pale pink lips.

"Fine," Brackmeyer said impatiently, "I don't care what you do with the little buggers."

The hag cackled triumphantly, clapping her hands together, and glided out of the cave, Brackmeyer close behind her. Now was their chance.

Henry and Linxz climbed through the window and into the cave. Linxz cut Wally's ropes, freeing him at once.

"Thanks," Wally exclaimed.

"We've got to get out of here," said Linxz, his face marked with worry.

"We need to find out what this machine is," said Henry. "If we don't, there will be no more Factory or Sweet Lands for that matter."

Henry, Linxz, and Wally tip-toed out of the cave and through the endless passageways that led through the mountain, following the echoing cackles and grunts of Brackmeyer and Anise. Moments later they were standing outside an enormous cave. A large machine, twice the size of any other that Henry had ever seen, glittered and gleamed in the dimly lit room.

Henry watched as Brackmeyer the ogre stroked the gray giant as if it were a pet.

"This machine," Anise reported, "can create an army the likes of which the Sweet Lands has never known."

"How does it work?" asked Brackmeyer, eagerly.

The hag walked over to a large control panel where a row of buttons sat. She pushed a large red one that instantly caused the machine to sputter and whir, belching great puffs of hot white steam from its protruding pipes. Henry had to stifle a gasp as several gingerbread men, the size of fully-grown elves, popped out at the other end.

Brackmeyer inspected the gingerbread men closely. "They're cookies!" he shouted, unconvinced that a cookie army could do much of anything but be eaten.

Anise whispered a few instructions to one of the gingerbread men. It sprang to life, walked over to the ogre, and lifted him clear off his feet with one hand.

"You see," she said, grinning wickedly "these are not just ordinary cookies. You can put him down now!" she commanded. The gingerbread man obeyed, dropping the ogre onto his furry backside before falling back into line with the rest of the cookie-soldiers.

"I must admit," grunted Brackmeyer, getting gingerly to his feet and rubbing his bottom, "I am impressed."

"You haven't seen anything yet," said the Anise.

The Hag turned another dial and pressed another button. Instantly the machine began to whiz and sputter. The gingerbread men reentered through a large opening on the side. When they re-emerged they were glistening.

"What is that stuff on them?" asked Brackmeyer.

"It is a protective coating. It will take a lot to destroy these cookies now!" her cackle filled the room. "Tomorrow we will be ready to march onto the Sweet Lands, REVENGE!"

At that moment something small and black flew over Henry's and Wally's head and into the cave. It swooped and dived around Anise, squeaking incessantly. Henry could just make out that the small creature was a black licorice bat, and if those squeaks were what Henry thought they were, they were in big, big trouble.

"What's this?" said the hag, turning to the bat, "thank you, my pet. Well, this is very interesting."

Brackmeyer, half listening, was still examining the machine.

"Dunkel tells me that there are three spies lurking in the tunnel, just outside this cave."

"What?" Brackmeyer croaked, looking up at last.

Henry tapped Wally and Linxz on the shoulder, gesturing that they had better leave. Just as they did, however, Henry heard the hag yell.

"Get them. Bring them to me!" Anise shrieked.

Running for their lives, Henry, Wally and Linxz took a tunnel to the left and found, much too late, that it led out onto a tight ledge. Still miles from the ground, Henry could see the jagged candy rocks, and the white foam of the Ice Cream Sea below.

The only way down was back through the cave. The thundering footsteps of three gingerbread patrolmen closed in on them. If they went back they would be caught for sure. They were trapped. On the ledge, Henry spotted a lone licorice tree.

Its vines of long black shoestrings hung from every branch. He had an idea. Henry quickly grabbed several very long pieces and tied them tightly together.

He gave one end to Wally.

"Quick, tie one end around the base of the tree."

Henry stood at the opposite end.

"Okay, Linxz," said Henry, "I need you to lure them out. When you are safely out of the cave, I will pull on the rope and make them trip and fall off the cliff."

"B-but …."

"No buts, Linxz, it's either that or be eaten by Anise!"

"Well, when you put it like that. Wish me luck."

Linxz, who was stiff with terror, entered the cave. The three gingerbread men that had been chasing them skidded to a stop looking around to see where they had gone.

"Hey, pea brains, here I am. Come and get me!" yelled Linxz, who was shaking his apple-size bottom at the gingerbread men.

The gingerbread men ran at full speed toward the little elf. Linxz continued to taunt them. They were getting closer now. Henry could see their frosted eyes and mouths piped into a frown. Linxz ran out onto the ledge, followed closely by the gingerbread soldiers. Henry only had a second to pull on the rope. He did. The first gingerbread man out tripped over it, causing the other two behind him to tumble over the other. The three went crashing over the narrow cliff, shattering into tiny pieces on the rocks below.

"That was close," said Linxz, panting and clutching his chest. "Let's get out of here before she sends anymore."

They crept back quietly through the cave, keeping a sharp eye out for more gingerbread soldiers and that bat.

CHAPTER THIRTEEN

A Very Sticky End

Once out of the mountain they started for Treacle Swamp. Linxz led them to a sparse area that had a lot of light and a great view of the mountain in case they were being followed.

Exhausted from all the running the three stopped for a brief moment to catch their collected breaths. Henry spotted a large boulder to sit upon, and forgetting where he was, accidentally stepped in a large sticky puddle. Almost at once there arose from the pool a large behemoth of dark heavy molasses. Henry, Wally, and Linxz stood glued to the spot as the giant rose higher and higher.

"Who are you?" it bellowed in a very low tone, like an old vinyl record played on the wrong speed. "Why do you trespass in my swamp? Come to steal my precious treacle, perhaps?" It fixed its single huge eye on them, unblinkingly.

"Oh, n-no sir," Linxz stammered, "We've just come from the mountain where Anise, the swamp hag, resides."

"ANISE?" roared the monster, rising even higher in its pool "what business have you with her?"

"No business at all," said Henry, quickly. "She and an ogre called Brackmeyer are planning to destroy the Sweet Lands."

The monster paused as his one large eye looked blearily at each of them.

"So, Anise has returned, has she? I have waited a very long time to get even with that hag!" It said acrimoniously.

It moved forward, dripping large dollops of its sticky body onto the ground at their feet.

"So you don't like her either," said Wally, somehow more at ease with the giant than the other two. "What did she do to you?" he asked.

It looked a bit surprised to be asked such a question, but seeing the look of sincerity on all their faces, decided to tell them.

"It's a very sad story," It said. "Pull up a boulder and I will tell you."

They did as it asked. The monster sank half way into the pool so that it was eye level with Henry, Wally, and Linxz.

"We treacle people are a peaceful lot. We kept to the great pond and ourselves mostly. Occasionally we would come out and trade with the elves from the Sweet Lands. In exchange for our treacle to make sweets, the elves built a small sugar-refining station, which produced more treacle to replenish our pond. All was harmonious until…," a short pause, then, its voice trembling with rage, continued. "Three hags came to the Sweet Lands, bringing darkness to our precious swamp. We tried to fight them but their magic was much too strong. They destroyed the sugar-refining station and tortured and killed many of my people, causing them to dry up and crystallize. A few others like me managed to escape. Where the others are now, I do not know." Its gigantic eye swelled with sugary tears. "They found me sometime later, crystallizing and near death. They cast a powerful spell over the swamp and imprisoned me in this small pool. I was doomed to serve as their sentry."

"How horrible," said Wally "Is there anything we can do to help you?"

"Alas," the monster sighed, "there is nothing you can do. If I leave this pool, I will dry up."

"There may be a way to defeat Anise, Brackmeyer, and her army of gingerbread soldiers, and break the spell that imprisons you," said Henry, now pacing back and forth. "But we will need your help."

"Anything to rid the swamp of that hag once and for all," said the monster.

"Good, I have an idea," said Henry.

When Henry, Wally, and Linxz returned to the Gumdrop Patrol encampment they found Mac, Emlin, and Captain Ogglebog in the tent discussing plans of the impending attack on the village. Linxz had radioed ahead with a full blown report on Anise's return, and her and Brackmeyer's gingerbread army.

Henry told them of their meeting with the Treacle Swamp monster and the plan he devised to stop the hag and Brackmeyer from entering the village.

"And you're certain it will help us?" asked Captain Ogglebog.

"Certain," said Henry, "It hates Anise just as much as we do."

"Then it's settled," said the captain, fastening a few buttons on his uniform, and adjusting the peppermint scabbard that hung at his side. "We will need at least fifty troops in the swamp. If we can take out a good portion of those cookie soldiers, we'll be a lot better off."

"Good, I'll help," Henry said.

"As will I," said Wally.

Henry had almost forgotten that his friend was still with them.

"No!" said Henry sharply, "you need to get back to your world."

"You can't expect me to leave now, not when my friends are in trouble, when they need me."

"You've already been here way too long, Wally," said Henry, placing a hand on Wally's shoulders. "Besides, Katie will kill me if we keep you here any longer."

"Katie, the children!" said Wally, slapping his hand to his forehead. "I almost forgot."

"You see, it's already happening. You're forgetting. That's why you have to leave. Tell me, did you eat or drink anything?"

Wally thought for a moment. "No," he replied.

"Excellent, you won't be affected as I was."

He saw Wally back through the tunnel and into the main cave, which led to the outside world. When the cave opened their first view was Katie. Henry had Mac radio ahead so that she could meet Wally in the forest. Fortunately for Wally, only a month had gone by instead of several years.

Katie, Heinrich and Gretchen stood next to the van wearing long heavy coats, scarves, and hats. Another heavy coat was tucked under Katie's arm as she walked forward toward Wally.

"Dad!" cried the children, rushing toward him.

Wally embraced his children. He looked up at Katie.

"Hi," he said softly, half -smiling, as his children held on tightly to him.

"Hi," she said softly, her blue eyes welling with happy tears. "Thought you might need this," she said, handing Wally his coat.

Wally pried his arms free from his children's embraces, took the coat and pulled it on, not taking his eyes off her. He finally was set free from Heinrich's and Gretchen's hugs and was able to greet Katie properly. He put his arms around her and kissed her tenderly. Henry looked on. He smiled and allowed himself a moment to enjoy the scene. But only a moment.

"I'm sorry to interrupt," he said, abruptly, and there was urgency in his voice now. "I have to be getting back."

"Henry, I want you to promise to keep us informed on the war. Should you need us, call!"

Henry nodded his promise, turned, and retreated back into the cave. He returned to find preparations for the war were in full swing. Large barricades of peppermint stalks jutted out of the ground at an angle all around the perimeter of the village, their pointed ends a dangerous deterrent. The Sweet Lands factory no longer produced sweets instead it had become a weapons-manufacturing plant; producing peppermint clubs and staves, licorice whips, candy spears and shields, and a bunch of other things to defend themselves against Anise's gingerbread menace.

A large catapult was being erected in the center of the village, to be wheeled into battle. Several tents, set up to help the injured, were pitched inside the village. Henry, Mac, and Emlin sat with Captain Ogglebog in the command tent, going over last minute details of their strategy.

"Henry, our team will engage the enemy here." He pointed to a spot on the map, the very spot where they had met the Treacle creature. "There's plenty of light there so she won't get the sneak on us. We must do whatever we can to lead her to us. Most of the team is there now setting up."

The sun reached high in the sky and a foreboding gloom seemed to overshadow the village. Every villager was armed to the tooth with their weapons, waiting at his or her post for the signal to attack.

Henry and Captain Ogglebog gathered the rest of their team and headed out in the direction of the swamp. "We'll be in touch." Henry said, giving Mac and Emlin a furtive smile and wink before starting off.

"Remember now, they are tough little cookies," the captain was saying some time later, "They'll have some sort of protective coating. If anything, aim for their legs. This will stop them in their tracks if not slow their advance."

A great hush fell over the swamp now as Henry, the captain and fifty other elves took their positions around the large sticky pool. Then in the distance Henry could hear the soft rumblings of footfalls drawing near. Closer and closer they came, the noise getting louder and louder. The ground trembled violently beneath their feet as fifty gnarly little gingerbread men, armed with peppermint bayonets, came marching into view.

"Do not attack until you see the icing around their eyes," shouted Captain Ogglebog to his troops, "Steady... steady, steady... NOW!!"

The elfin army advanced on the gingerbread men like a swarm of honey bees as they came into the target area, but the gingerbread soldiers knocked handful after handful of elves out of the way

The elves fought gallantly, taking out dozens of gingerbread soldiers by any means necessary, but in spite of their efforts they were just no match for them. Anise's army proved to be a formidable foe. Large numbers of elves dropped like swatted flies. They were losing.

Henry, armed with his peppermint staff and shield, did the best he could to bring the gingerbread shoulders closer to the sticky pool. There was just too many of them. Then a high-pitched whistle rang out over the swamp, making the gingerbread army stop dead in its tracks. They stood at attention. Henry and the others stopped too.

"Seize them," hissed the voice of the hag, making her way over a few battle scared gingerbread men, and several injured elves, followed by the erratic flight of her pet bat, Dunkel.

Several gingerbread soldiers sprang forward and bound the remaining elves left standing. The others formed two rows opposite one another, as if in a royal ceremony.

Henry looked around. Brackmeyer was nowhere to be seen.

"Captain Ogglebog," the old hag croaked, as she walked through her imperial cookie guardsmen, like royalty. "We meet again. I have been waiting a very long time for this." She began to pace back and forth not taking those menacingly dark eyes off of him. "How do you like my army? I'm sure you've found out that their candy coating is virtually impossible to break?"

"What do you want, Anise?" Captain Ogglebog said as calmly as he could possibly manage.

Henry saw those thin pale lips curled in a vicious grin revealing her sharp teeth and poisonous green tongue. She walked slowly up to Captain Ogglebog and stooped down so that she was eye level.

"You know why I've come."

"Refresh my memory," said the captain, backing away from Anise.

The hag continued her icy stare. "I've come to avenge my sisters." She drew closer to the captain and ran a long, sharp claw-like finger down the side of the elf's face, and stuck it in her mouth. "Sweet and tender you'll be, once you are stuffed properly." She began to drool. It looked like she was about to bite him. And in fact her face was moving ever closer to the Captain's, her mouth open, her teeth dripping with saliva.

Henry had to act before Captain Ogglebog became lunch for the hag. He broke free of his gingerbread captor, tearing his shirt in the process, and stood next to the large treacle pool. The hag's attention moved swiftly in his direction. Once again her lips curled in a horrible grin. "Ah, Henry Peppermint Twist, what a meal you would have made for my sisters. They preferred the taste of human flesh to elf, really. But they are no longer with us. No matter, someone else wants the pleasure of destroying you."

"And where is the Brackmonster anyway? Abandoned you, did he?" Henry asked defiantly.

"He'll be along presently, never-you-mind," she snarled. "Detain him!" she spat. "And now for a little unfinished business...." She turned once again to Captain Ogglebog, licking her lips greedily.

"You'll never get away with this, Anise! Our army...."

"Your army ...?" Anise cackled "Your army? Your army my dear, sweet captain is no match for mine, as you have clearly seen!"

"I wouldn't bet on that," said Henry, trying desperately to distract the Swamp Hag and keep her from taking a bite out of the Captain. He whistled and up from its glutinous pond rose the swamp monster. It appeared twice as large and twice as menacing as Henry had seen it before. Anise stopped laughing as the monster immediately cemented the feet of the hags gingerbread army with huge amounts of sticky molasses that shot from its fingertips.

"I command you to stop!" she cried.

But the creature had already fallen upon the cookies. When it arose, the entire gingerbread army was stuck to its body.

"Remember me?" it growled, lowering itself a bit into its small gummy prison.

Anise tried to flee, but another quick blast from the monsters fingers cemented her arms and feet to the swamp floor.

"Revenge is very sweet," said the monster and in an instant she was scooped up into its sticky embrace.

"This is not over yet, you miserable fools!" she shrieked, as the monster began to lower itself back into the pool, dragging the hag along with it.

"You're finished, Anise!" said captain Ogglebog, grinning.

"Before this day is over," said the hag, who was now up to her neck in treacle, and sinking fast, "I will have the last laugh." And with a 'plop' she was gone, lost beneath the viscid abyss that was her tomb.

Once the last of the bubbles had faded, the monster rose again. A deep sigh of relief, followed by cheers of triumph. Before their eyes, the entire swamp began to transform. The spell was broken at last.

Henry watched as the darkness that completely enveloped the entire swamp was swept away by the wind. The monsters treacle prison also transformed, elongating to join with the main pond deep inside the swamp.

"Thank you, my friends," the monster gurgled as it moved up the sticky river and out of sight. "Thank yoooou …!"

With Anise finally gone from the Sweet Lands forever, their attentions turned to Brackmeyer? Why didn't he come to the hag's aid? Had he doubled crossed her? A trait most familiar to Henry of his old employer.

They quickly made haste back to the village, helping the injured elves through the swampland.

"What's the matter?" asked Captain Ogglebog, noticing Henry's worried expression. But he soon learned "what." Before reaching the entrance to the village the ground all around them began to rumble and shake more violently than the last.

Henry spun around and to his horror he saw it. From the swamp emerged a colossal gingerbread man. It stood as tall as two gingerbread factory's and was flanked by fifty more nasty little gingerbread soldiers. High aloft on the beast's wide cookie shoulders sat the ogre, Brackmeyer, his face full of anger and hatred bubbling in his heart.

Henry watched as he motioned his soldiers forward. . . onward. . . to war!

CHAPTER FOURTEEN

The War Continues

THUD, THUD, THUD, went the thundering footsteps of the giant gingerbread beast as it moved swiftly across the land towards the elves defensive line. Elves scampered in every direction, trying to stay clear of its massive feet, which hit the ground like ten-ton boulders causing it to quake.

Henry, Mac, and Captain Ogglebog quickly reorganised the troops and began their assault on the cookie army.

"Give it up, Twist!" Brackmeyer hollered from above. "You can't possibly win this."

The colossal gingerbread beast and its tiny army plowed through the front line of the elfin defense like a sharp knife cutting through cookie dough. Injured elves were being carried off to infirmary tents left and right. Emlin and several of the other elves who worked in these hospital tents were kept very busy cleaning cuts and bruises, and bandaging broken arms and legs. Their army was dwindling fast. The protective coating that was shielding the cookie army was withstanding the elfin assault no matter what they threw at it.

The situation was looking very grim, indeed. All seemed lost as the colossal gingerbread man plowed through another elfin barrier that led to the Sweet Land Factory.

"We have to stop it before it reaches the factory," howled Mac in desperation.

Amid the panicked voices, Henry was struck with an idea. Why hadn't he thought of this before? It was so simple.

"Milk!" he shouted, "We need lots of milk."

Mac frowned, a puzzled expression on his face. "How can you be thirsty at a time like this?"

"It's not for me," said Henry, knocking an advancing cookie soldier to the ground with his peppermint staff. "I want to use it on the gingerbread army. If we soften them up a bit, we may be able to stop them."

"Brilliant!" said Mac, "I'll see to it."

It seemed like an eternity.

"Where are they with that milk?" cried Henry, looking frantically around for Mac and the Captain.

Moments later, Mac, Captain Ogglebog and two other elves wheeled into position a large vat of milk. And not a moment too soon, as the cookie army was pushing through the elfin line of defense.

"When I give the word," shouted Henry, breaking free and running over to the vat, "give those cookies a good soaking. READY..., FIRE!"

Milk shot from the hose with the force of a bullet. The cookies that were hit directly broke in two. Gingerbread soldiers fell back. The milk did exactly what Henry had hoped: softened the cookies protective coating so that the elves would be able to finish them off. One by one soggy gingerbread men fell to the ground with a soft 'flump.'

More soaked cookies sank to the ground as the milk spray continued. Henry and the elves fought with new found strength. The tide was turning; they were winning at last.

Brackmeyer, seething with anger, urged the giant onward toward the factory. The monster loomed dangerously over the factory and waited for Brackmeyer's instruction. "You miserable little imps, thought you could defeat Me." shouted

Brackmeyer as the last of his gnarly cookie army flopped to the ground.

Henry ran forward. As he got closer he could see the deranged look on the ogre's face.

"Say goodbye to your precious factory, Twist!"

The ogre shouted his command into the giant's ear. Slowly the colossal beast lifted its massive arms, and in one fell swoop, brought them crashing down upon the factory's thatched roof. Elves advanced on the giant throwing whatever they could find at it. But nothing switched the giants focus from its main target. It raised its powerful arms again, poised for another devastating blow. Quickly, Henry grabbed the hose and aimed it directly at the monsters raised arms, soaking them thoroughly with milk.

"Keep it up Henry!" Mac shouted "It's starting to work!"

The monsters arms began to break apart in small bits. But this was a big cookie. Brackmeyer swore bitterly and instructed the giant to use its feet. It turned and advanced.

"Crush them!" The ogre yelled. "Squash the nasty little vermin!"

Henry immediately turned the hose and aimed it at the giant cookie's legs. He adjusted the nozzle so that the milk sprayed in a steady stream, but in the excitement of the battle Henry hadn't noticed that the milk was running out.

"More pressure!" Henry shouted. None came. Seconds later, they had run completely out.

"There's no more milk," cried Captain Ogglebog, shaking with fear. "Not one drop left in the whole village."

"Well, that's it then," said Mac, looking grim. "We've had it. We're doomed!"

The giant advanced, picking up its mammoth legs to step on the elves, who scattered like bugs beneath its elephantine feet.

"We need to give the milk more time to soak in," said Henry, moving in the nick of time as the giants foot came crashing down in the spot where he stood. "I soaked it pretty good. If we can impede its movements, it may be all the time we'll need for the milk to soften his legs."

"A diversion," Captain Ogglebog said, rolling out of the way, next to Mac and Henry. "It's worth a try."

Captain Ogglebog got quickly to his feet and called his troops together. They formed into ranks. "Okay, just like we practiced it. C7!"

The Gumdrop patrol formed their pyramid. The colossal gingerbread man froze as did Brackmeyer. They gazed confusedly down at the tiny elfin triangle. Next minute the pyramid broke apart and the elves were flipping and somersaulting around the giant's feet, throwing spears and hitting it with clubs.

Unable to stamp on the miniature acrobats, the gingerbread colossus let out a roar of frustration.

Brackmeyer shouted, jumping up and down in a blinding fury on the giant's shoulders.

"No, no, no, you big stupid cookie," a frustrated Brackmeyer vociferated from above. But the cookie ignored the ogre. It chased after the little elves, trying to pick them up with his enormous gingerbread fingers. But it couldn't, its fingers were much too rigid. The elves laughed as they led the cookie beast further and further away from the factory and village.

They continued their flipping and somersaulting for some time, but even elves get weary.

"Ha," said the ogre as the elves fell away at last. "Look at them. They're tiring out."

The elves had finally stopped. They lay sprawled out over the grounds, trying to catch their breath. Brackmeyer laughed. Once again he and the giant turned toward the factory.

"Nice try, Twist!" The ogre said with a triumphant smile. "You brought yourself a brief moment. Thought you'd put me out of business with your little sweet shop?" He continued to peer down at them from his giant gingerbread perch. "After I destroy the factory, I will lay waste to this little faerie-land of yours. Then we'll see who's …" He stopped talking. His mouth half opened as he looked in the direction of the Peppermint Forest.

Henry wheeled around too, so did Mac and the other elves. A soft rumbling, like the sound of stampeding trifles, came thundering over the hill.

Seventy-five children, led by Heinrich and Gretchen, rushed into view. Wally, Katie and Emlin followed closely behind them.

"Surround the giant!" Gretchen called out.

"Bite his legs off!" Heinrich yelled.

The children reached the giant gingerbread man, and like a pack of ravenous wolves, began breaking off large chunks of the cookie's legs. The milk had softened them up sufficiently so that colossus was more cake than cookie.

Brackmeyer was livid. He pulled great tufts of hair from his hairy head and screeched in a much higher voice than usual.

"You there, back away! Get away you nasty little urchins!"

The giant gingerbread wobbled and swayed this way and that. Children ran up to it in turn, hacking off great pieces of its legs, and then retreating with their prize.

"Stop that!" Brackmeyer continued to yell. "Stop that or I will squash you!"

The giant rocked unsteadily on its feet then finally fell to earth, shattering into a hundred pieces. Brackmeyer was thrown several yards over. The children, acting as all children would when such a treat lands at their feet, scrambled excitedly to collect the shards of cookie.

Wally, Katie, and Emlin approached Henry, Mac, and Captain Ogglebog.

"I thought we could use some reinforcements," said Emlin.

"And just in time, too," said Captain Ogglebog.

Henry beamed at Emlin. She smiled back as her soft red hair fell gently over her face and sparkling left green eye.

"But where on earth did all these children come from?" asked Henry.

"Got them from an Orphanage up the road from the retirement home," said Wally. "It was the kid's idea, Heinrich and Gretchen. The city was about to shut it down. Katie and I saved it. We decided to take the children out on a little outing of sorts."

"Brilliant!" said Henry.

"Inspired!" said Mac.

They turned and watched the children munching away on the cookie parts.

A loud roar issued over the landscape, as the ogre came lumbering toward the encampment. Children scrambled to get out of his way.

"TWIST!" boomed the loud voice of Brackmeyer, as he stood in the center of the village holding a large peppermint staff, his eyes wild, and his body shaking with frenzied anger.

Henry turned and faced the ogre.

"What do you want Brackmeyer?"

"You," he growled. "I just want you!"

Heinrich handed Henry a staff as Brackmeyer advanced, swinging his wildly. All eyes watched as the peppermint staves came together. They clanged and clashed, glowing with neon brilliance as they struck blows. Brackmeyer swung with such tremendous force that Henry was knocked to the ground several times.

"The game is up!" Brackmeyer said, looming over Henry like a dark cloud. "Did you really think you and your little friends could defeat me? You? You're not really a child, just a miserable old man!"

Henry didn't move. He had even stopped listening. All he could do was watch as a furious Brackmeyer raged on with his arms flapping and his big, hairy feet stomping. If Henry didn't know any better, the Ogre that was Brackmeyer was having an old fashioned temper tantrum. As the ogre's temper crescendo'ed into the stratosphere, Henry let out a snicker, then another, till soon he found he was laughing so hard he could barely breathe.

Brackmeyer stopped his tirade at once, looking confused. The elves too were looking at Henry strangely, wondering what on earth had gotten into him.

For a brief moment it looked as if the fight was over. But a very large vein in Brackmeyer's temple was throbbing and his left eye began to twitch. With a loud roar of fury the ogre swung his staff more violently. But this time it was Henry that caught the ogre off guard and sent him crashing to the ground.

"You will never be one of them, Twist. You're just a miserable old man that nobody wants!" spat Brackmeyer, acidly.

"Don't listen to him, Henry," Emlin hollered, "He is trying to trick you."

But Henry did listen and he remembered. His face fell as he recalled losing everything he loved. His heart sank as he remembered moving from his beloved home in Apfeldorf to live out the rest of his days in a retirement home in the country, a useless, old man.

It was all the edge Brackmeyer needed. With one swift, but very powerful blow, the ogre's staff had once again knocked Henry off his feet, almost knocking him headlong into a large hole in the ground that was used for garbage.

The ogre that was Brackmeyer advanced slowly. "Pathetic!" he said, glowering over Henry. "I did well by letting you go, Twist. My work is done here."

Battered and bruised, Henry sat there taking in all of the devastation around him. Brackmeyer had won. *Maybe he was right,* Henry thought. *"Maybe he would never be one of them, a real elf."* He hung his head, avoiding the tiny eyes that were on him now.

But something caught his ears causing Henry to look up at once. The elves were gathering around him, whispering something. Their words were surrounding him, filling him, and only him: feeding him words of encouragement, and hope, and love. He looked into Emlin's emerald eyes. She smiled and nodded as she continued her whisperings of: "You are ageless," "I believe in you, Henry," and, "I love you!" The other elves kept up their quiet chanting. "You will always be one of us!" and "You will never be old!" This melted sweetly into his mind and took hold. Like a soothing balm, their words energized Henry.

"Yes"! He thought, and his smile broke the mesmerizing grip that age had over him. At once a change took place deep inside him. It was the feeling of vitality, the very reflection of youth.

Energy surged throughout his entire body like lightening and he quickly got to his feet. Henry stood erect, looking much different than he had before. He didn't feel so old anymore. Different memories flooded his thoughts now, spurred on by the whispering elves around him. A new word reached his ears -- *Remember!*

And Henry did remember. The many times he spent with his mother and grandmother in the kitchen baking, and his early days at Brackmeyer Sweets. Warmth began to flood his entire being. He felt as if he had drunk a goblet full of Oozleberry wine laced with Bongo Buds. The pain that he felt from battle had gone too. He bullied his brain to except the fact that he was young again! He stood there defiantly glaring at Brackmeyer

"Correction, old man," Henry said defiantly, "it is you that is pathetic."

Brackmeyer who had started walking out of the village, stopped in his tracks and turned to face Henry, who it seemed was positively glowing with new found vigor.

"What did you say to me, boy?" snapped the ogre.

"Losing your hearing?" Henry teased.

"Why you insolent little pup ...!"

Brackmeyer, beside himself with rage leapt forward to attack, but this time Henry was ready. With the agility and swiftness of an elf, he simply side-stepped the ogre, sticking out his staff, which caused Brackmeyer to trip over his own big hairy feet. He stumbled forward. As quick as thought Henry turned and whacked the ogre on his backside, taking advantage of his forward momentum, and sent him tumbling headlong into the garbage pit.

Everyone watched as the ogre spiraled down, down, down, until he was lost altogether in the black nothingness. To Henry's surprise, the hole began to shrink. It got smaller and smaller and smaller, and then, with a small pop, disappeared. It was over at last.

Henry sat for a moment as his adrenaline subsided, bringing back the aching muscles and the worn out feeling from the fighting. When he finally looked up Emlin was at his side attending to his bruises. She applied a series of salves and ointments, which smelled strongly of cocoa and mint, instantly soothing his stinging cuts. He smiled at her and touched the side of her delicate face.

They saw the orphaned children safely through the tunnel and back into the human world. Henry watched as the children ran off excitedly. Their boundless supply of energy still amazed him. It reminded him, once again of his own youth.

"But I'm not old!" he exclaimed vehemently in his own mind. This was true. Even though Henry had aged while living in the human world, he still felt that spark that was, and is forever, youth burning in his heart. It was this feeling that was the source of his creativity and the reason he continued to feel young and energetic while at Brackmeyer Sweets, and it was this feeling, turned into magic, that had transformed him into his younger self when entering the Sweet Lands. "But I'm puzzled. Why didn't the children change?" he asked Emlin.

"They ate a giant gingerbread cookie."

"Ah," whispered Emlin, "children hold within them the magic of faerie. Their hearts are pure, and because they truly believe, they will always be able to see faeries."

"A profound statement," Henry thought. It made him feel truly young again in spirit.

"So, Ben was right all along then," he said to Emlin, watching the children make their way to two school buses that waited for them in the forest, "You really are as young as you think or feel."

He looked at Emlin, who continued to smile, reassuringly. She placed her hand in his as the cave entrance began to close.

CHAPTER FIFTEEN

The Sweet Life

It was a busy time in the Sweet Lands. A brand new factory was being built, a bit larger than the last. With the help of Anise's cookie machine, and a bit of tinkering from Gobo the elf, hundreds of gingerbread laborers were able to work around the clock. And they would need the extra space, as Henry's brain was already working overtime coming up with sweet new ideas.

He felt a certain peace now. Though Henry knew that in human years he was well over one hundred, it did not change the way he saw himself, young and useful. At last he could do what he loved without the fear of growing old. In fact he was starting to feel less human and more like an elf every day. He found himself working out with the Gumdrop Patrol; flipping and somersaulting into tricky formations. On other days he helped Zandlor in the forest by planting new saplings, or cutting down only the ones marked for the mill. Henry became much a part of the Sweet Lands as any elf. But something was still gnawing at him in the back of his mind. Something that had bothered him those many years ago, when he watched his friend being led away in the night.

"Mac," said Henry, one afternoon as they skipped jawbreakers over the chocolate pond, "I've been meaning to ask you something. What ever happened to Ben and all of the people from the retirement home that came here before me?"

"Oh them," said Mac, smiling wryly. "Well, Henry some boarded a ship that took them to other Islands. Some stayed here with us. You met some of them. Minkle, Captain Ogglebog, Linxz. They all took different names, of course; Elfin names."

"And what about Ben," Henry asked eagerly,

"Ben?" said the elf, looking puzzled.

"Yes, Ben, the man that came here right before I did." Henry explained.

"Oh, Ben, yes, well he became the captain of the S.S. Popillol. He doesn't go by Ben anymore, though. He prefers to be called Captain Maerc."

Henry snickered. He knew at once that 'Popillol' and 'Maerc' weren't really words at all, but 'Lollipop' and 'Cream' spelled in reverse.

Twist Treats continued to flourish. Soon the great crowds that came to visit were too much for the little shop. It was decided that a new shop, one that could accommodate the larger numbers, would have to be built. But where?

"How about where the retirement home used to be?" Katie suggested. She had just recently inherited everything from her missing uncle's estate.

"That's a great idea," said Wally, excitedly. "For many reasons," he continued, lowering his voice so as not to be heard.

"We can use the money we got from the sale of factory. I hear they are tearing it down tomorrow." Katie added, looking a bit forlorn. It had, after all, been her family's legacy.

Wally put an arm around his wife, consolingly.

"Maybe we can salvage a few things that have been lost," Wally suggested.

"Like what?" asked Katie; brushing back a few tears.

"How about we hire some of the workers back. We are building a bigger shop and we'll need to hire more people."

Katie looked at her husband with gratitude in her eyes. She hugged and kissed him as if she hadn't seen him in years. It was just the thing she needed to hear at that moment.

As the years rolled further along and Wally and Katie reached their seventies, they decided it was time to retire. They left the shop in the hands of their children, Heinrich and Gretchen, who were now old enough with families of their own.

The one thing they insisted, however, was to continue to go with them whenever they made supply runs. This gave them a chance to talk to Henry and Emlin. The topic of discussion mainly was their retirement into the Sweet Lands and the immediate construction of their own gingerbread house, which would be ready just in time for their arrival in the next year.

With the plans for his friend's arrival on schedule and the success of Twist Treats at its new location near the dark forest of Cratzenbach, Henry turned his attention to different matters. He and Emlin were beginning to spend an awful lot of time together. They ate together, picked Bongo Buds and Oozleberries together. Each waking moment spent with Emlin was filled with fun and laughter. It was something that Henry never wanted to end.

As he lay in his floating bed recounting the adventures he just had with the elves, his success with Twist Treats, and his blossoming relationship with Emlin, he wondered what other new and exciting things this new world would unfold. Life in the Sweet Lands, so far, had been a great adventure. He turned over and closed his eyes, thinking *"this a perfect ending to a sweet life"* – that, in his mind, just got a bit sweeter.

Epilogue

Though Henry's life was indeed a bit sweeter, having lived over two hundred of his human years in the Sweet Lands, his life and adventures were far from over.

An elf from the Gumdrop Patrol had turned up at the Sweet Lands Factory with a letter one morning, looking distressed. Apparently the cargo ship, the S.S. Popillol, and its entire crew, had gone missing while on a routine supply run. This meant that their supply of milk, butter, eggs, flour, honey and a bunch of other items were dangerously low. For these much needed supplies a trip across the Ice Cream Sea to a series of smaller Islands, Henry had never seen before, was in order.

Under normal circumstances, Henry would have looked forward to visiting these other islands, but the letter also carried with it news about a growing conflict; a conflict which was escalating into war between two territories on the Island of Milk and Honey.

Queen Moo ruled the territory of Milk in the north. She was a very kind queen, and her cows were always well fed and content. All of the milk, cream, and butter used in the Sweet Lands came from her territory.

In the south, where the weather was warmer, sat the territory of Honey. There, Queen Sweet Sting ruled on her honeycombed throne of gold. She wasn't as nice as Queen Moo, in fact she was a tyrant. She worked her drones to near exhaustion, having them build elaborate hives with several chambers to house, not her offspring, but her many mirrors, for she was a very vain queen who insisted on being told how beautiful she was at every moment. Not to pay such a tribute was dangerous.

Wasting no time, a new crew was assembled. A new ship, much bigger than the Popillol, was built out of an enormous boiled-sweet. Captain Ogglebog, Mac, Henry, and Emlin along with eleven members of the Gumdrop patrol, set sail as soon as they were able. Their first destination: Sugar Island.

"We will follow the same route as the Popillol," Captain Ogglebog announced and he traced his finger along a worn route on his sea map. "Gathering supplies, as well as clues to the crew's whereabouts."

"How bad is the conflict?" asked Henry.

"Pretty bad. I've had dealings with the Queen before in the land of Honey. A right piece of work, she is; her words are as bad as her stings! We'll need to be on our guard. Try and stay on her good side."

Before Henry could wrap his mind entirely around the fact that he was about to meet a talking queen bee, and a talking bovine, He, Emlin and Mac were standing on the deck of the ship as it pulled slowly away from the harbour. Henry got a funny feeling in the pit of his stomach. He wasn't sure, but if things were really bad on these islands as it was reported, would he ever see the Sweet Lands again? But like every child, the prospect of exploring fantastical, far-away places, friendly or dangerous, intrigued him.

As he lay awake that night, turning over in his mind the new places he was about to explore and the supposed dangers that lay ahead for them all, never, in a million years, could he ever imagine such an ending for this master baker. But this was not the end of Henry Peppermint Twist. Not by a long shot. Mysterious forces were at work, once again, shaping events that would take him on yet another great life adventure. An adventure filled with places far stranger, and far more fantastic than he had already experienced.

And so the ship sailed on through the night, with Henry fast asleep, finally, dreaming wonderful dreams of faraway places, with Emlin and Mac, now sound asleep in their bunks, on a boat made entirely out of candy -- adrift on a very tranquil Ice Cream Sea.

Lebkuchen Haus (Gingerbread House)

Here is a great recipe for you to create your own versions of the gingerbread houses featured in this book.

Lebkuchen/Gingerbread

7 cups (1.7 L) unbleached, white whole wheat flour (withholding 1 cup/ .24 L)
1 teaspoon (5 mL) baking soda
½ teaspoon (2 mL) baking powder
1 cup (2 sticks / 250 mL) unsalted butter
1 ½ cups (375 mL) unsulphured molasses/treacle
1 cup (250 mL) dark-brown sugar
4 teaspoons (20 mL) ground Chinese ginger
4 teaspoons (20 mL) ground cinnamon
1 ½ teaspoons (7.5 mL) ground cloves
1 teaspoon (5 ml) ground allspice
2 large eggs (or 3 small ones) beaten

To make the gingerbread

Preheat oven 350°F (180°C)
1. In a saucepan heat butter, brown sugar and molasses over medium heat until butter is melted and sugar is dissolved – do not boil! Remove saucepan from the flame and let cool slightly.

2. In a large bowl, sift together 6 cups (1.7 L) flour, baking soda and baking powder, ginger, cinnamon, cloves and allspice. Sift the remaining 1 cup (250 mL) of flour and set aside.

3. Pour butter, brown sugar and molasses/treacle mixture, along with beaten eggs, into flour mixture. Mix together with a spoon until dough forms. Use your hands to work (knead) the dough. Add remaining 1 cup (250 mL) flour a bit at a time until dough is no longer sticky.

4. Divide dough in half and wrap in plastic. Refrigerate at least 1 hour, preferably overnight, until firm (dough can be made up to 1 week in advance. Just wrap in plastic and refrigerate).

5. On a well-floured surface, roll out dough to ¼ inch (5mm) thickness. It is best if you do this on a floured piece of baking parchment before you begin cutting your shapes. It will make moving the pieces onto the cookie sheet easier.

6. Using a template of your own design or using the example provided in this book, cut out the shapes of the house (2 gable pieces, 2 roof pieces, 2 wall pieces and if you prefer the 4 chimney pieces). Chill each piece until firm (15-20 minutes) Bake until firm (20 minutes for large pieces and 15 minutes for the small pieces).

Royal Icing

2 large egg whites (you may add more egg whites or substitute 5 tablespoons /75 mL of meringue powder and 1/3 cup / 75 mL of water to thin the icing). 4 cups (1 L) sifted icing sugar (you may add more to make thicker) and the juice from 1 lemon.

Using an electric hand mixer or stand mixer, beat egg whites until stiff but not dry. Add icing sugar and lemon juice. Beat for 10 minutes longer on high speed. Icing should be stiff and glossy and about as thick as toothpaste. If the icing is too thick ass more egg whites: if too thin add more sugar. Cover with damp towel and put off to the side until ready to use. This will be the glue to hold the pieces of the gingerbread house together.

To construct the Lebkuchen Haus/Gingerbread House

You will need a stiff piece of corrugated cardboard or a thin piece of plywood for your base about 18-20 inches square.

1. Spoon royal icing into pastry bag with medium round tip, or use a re-sealable freezer bag with less than ¼ inch (5 mm) off the tip of the bag. Remove all the air from bag.

    Keep the unused icing in a bowl covered with a damp towel. Also wrap a damp paper towel around the tip of the pastry bag when not in use.

2. Using the royal icing as a glue, stand the 4 walls of the house (supporting them with a cup or can) and glue them together using the royal icing. Let them dry for 25 minutes (icing will get hard). Remove the can. Attach the roof pieces, using the cup or can to prop them up. Let dry. Attach the chimney (optional) and let dry.

Make sure you remove the can when the pieces have dried properly.

3. Use icing to attach the house directly to the base. Let set till hard.

4. Finish your house by decorating it using the royal icing as the glue and lots of brightly colored candies and other edibles.

Lebkuchen Template

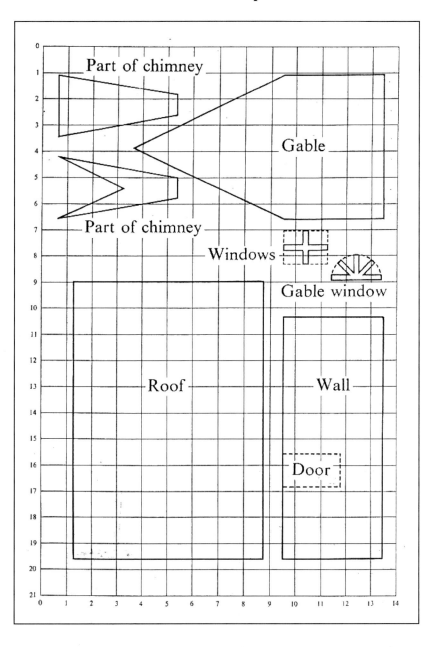

Edwards Brothers Malloy
Thorofare, NJ USA
May 10, 2016